DAPHNE OF THE
FOREST CLAN

ISBN: 978-1-969865-13-8 Paperback
ISBN: 978-1-969865-14-5 Ebook

Rev. date: 10/07/2025

DAPHNE OF THE FOREST CLAN

Douglas Nolan

CHAPTER I

The world that Daphne and her clan lived in a plain that is in a different world than that of any we know of. It is backwards from everything you think you knew. For we have a Blue sky however, in Daphne's plane, it is liquid, and it is red. When they look up in her world the sky changes colors and swirls around as it is being mixed up like a drink in a glass.

Her planet is called many things depending on where you would come from, for you see there have been many traveler's that wind up in their forest and they all claim to come from different worlds. She was told a story from her mother about how her clan came to this plain over a hundred thousand cycles ago. Her clan was given the task of protecting the Forests way back when the first protectors of the forest choose to leave this plain for, they found a way to leave to their new planet Wardaratia. It has been so long since anyone has said the name of our planet, said "Daphne" that I do not even remember anything about it. This has been our home for so long, over a thousand cycles, it is also were we first noticed we had powers. Each of our powers are different but, in many ways, the same, for we each are shape shifters and we all shift into an animal of the forest. We found out that there are rules to the kinds of shifting we could do; for number one; any animal in the woods or forest like Bears, Tigers, Wolves, Deer, and animals of this nature, nothing out side of the woods or forest.

No Lions, Cheetahs, Elephants, Hippos, and things of that sort are not possible. None of our shape shifting may cause bodily harm to any animal or any life form, or the person that caused the breaking will lose his/her powers for ever no exceptions, how this is done was a secret only the protectors had the knowledge of doing.

Also, we seem to live for an exceptionally long time if we are in good standings and have not killed anything while being a shape shifter on this plain.

We must take on human form to kill our food and fish for our meals, just to keep us on our toes I guess, so we do not forget who we are. For we may have all come to this place from different planets or plains, but we all normal until we somehow come to this place. Daphne looked at the sky and saw that a storm was brewing and that if she was going to get her chores done before the red sky started to pour down on her. She knew that she could do something to help her do her chores faster, but her mom; Linda of the Night Sage who, was in a meeting the last time when Daphne shifted into a large nosed winged bear bat. (What a mess she made) and it took her a fourth night to clean up what would have taken one or two spinning's of the lunar day. She was in a hurry today to get chores done so she could go out with her friend Wind Talker for she just graduated and received her new life name. Daphne could not wait, for she only had one more year herself if she could only stay out of trouble with the teachers at school, she got in the most trouble because she felt that they were wrong about the way they taught. For her mother had always explained their history differently, and her mother The Night Sage was gifted with the knowledge of the cycles before us. Her mother told her that she needed to listen to the teachers at school and then when she is old enough she would have her life name and being the daughter of the Night Sage, she would be very respected and honored. With the life name came what you would be chosen to be for the rest of your life; like with her older friends and clan members: Wind Talker, Bore Hunter, Storm Talker just to name a few. In the Forest, life is not easy you have to get up early to do your choirs, which details milking the cows, gathering the eggs for breakfast. All the while, the men are doing their choirs tending to the Horses and feeding the Pigs.

Hunting for meat to put on the table for breakfast or gutting it and drying it for the next day's dinner. Then the bell rang for school and I must run to get there on time, today we are learning how to control our powers better.

So that I do not have any more what it was called "a Long-Nosed bear bat" man did I get in trouble for that? Not only was I underage to use my shape shifting powers and I could not control it so instead of making my chores go by faster, I shifted something that was not of any plain.

Because it was such a serious act on my part, I was barred from going to Shifting School until my mother could bring it up to the Forest council. Only because of who my mother is the Night Sage of the Forest Clan that I got off with a warning, and a loss of two cycles banned from school. I cried for what seemed like a lunar period and then my mother called for me. She was in a council meeting and could not get away so, she sent Tree Mender to escort me to where the council was meeting and to keep me company until my mother was done with her meeting. Tree Mender was telling me about some of the sick trees that he was taking care of and how he gathered the right herbs in the forest the repair the trees in need of his herbs and healing powers. This all made my problems seem smaller after talking to Tree Mender and as I turned, my mother was standing behind us with a big smile on her face. So, you finely got over you are sulking about losing two cycles of shifting school, you are lucky you were not banned from the school, or the Forest all together. Yes, I am over my sulking mother, I was listening to Tree Mender and how he takes care of our forest it made my problems seem small. What did you call for me Mother? I talked to the council and they said that if you were on probation for one cycle and had no marks against her, she will be admitted into Shifting School. Daphne thought this was great one less cycle and all she had to do is stay out of trouble! She has never been able to stay out of trouble and that is why she was in this mess and the council new it.

This was a death sentence for she was a born troublemaker, well she was on to them if they all thought that they could pull her strings like a puppet then they were wrong. It would be hard but with her double checking what she did before she did it and with the help from her family, and friends she would show them, she would not let herself fall into their trap.

Back to the present day, in school we are learning to control our powers so that we do not have any problems like when we want to shift into a toad, we do not become a tadpole. We are taught to shift into trivial things to learn control, and then only after we have mastered the trivial things we go on to the bigger. The solar cycles that we waste, on this are not necessary said Daphne. She thought it was a waste of time, let us be real when are we going to need to turn into a toad. After school we have homework that we must practice for the solar days lesson plan, which is made easier with the help of a friend. My mother keeps telling me that we must learn how to control our powers to the smallest of animals in case we need to escape from a predator that can sense larger animals. My mother did not get her high seat on the council for being wrong, so I hit the books and learned as much as I could about shifting. After several cycles I was in the top of my class, and the council wanted to award me for my demanding work. I told you that I would not give them the satisfaction of my failing and the council thinking they we are right about me. Graduation was around the corner and I could not wait until the time for all the graduates to receive their life names. At school we were working on shifting into larger and larger animals each day. First, we worked on creatures that walked on the land and then we graduated to the flying an animal, learning to fly is harder than it looks. Getting the art of flight down pat is something that takes some finesse, let alone getting the air currents down is a pain in the ass. Of her practicing the end is near, the prize is within Daphne's sight and all she to do is history of the Clans and then the cycle would be over. With history on the line she went to her mother to ask her about the History of the Clans.

Her mother started out by saying that over a thousand cycles ago there were Four Clans, all at war with each other.

This meant that all four clans were at risk of dying off, if the "War of the Clans" lasted for more than a ten-cycle period. The Four Clans were once one Clan and over a thousand lunar cycles they started to pull apart over time. They started to use their shape shifting in war and for killing a shifter which was once not even thought of.

Killing became common place, a daily affair to kill, shifter against shifter, what was a population that many said they were as far as the forest and the sky, and the sea, even deserts. Now their numbers fall from the sky every solar day and lunar night. It was not safe to be a shifter, if you didn't want to be in the "War of the Clans" you would be killed unless you could hide in plain sight like being so small that no one could see you, maybe a tadpole in a small pond. Ok so I guess it can be important in a pinch, referring to her class lesson, Daphne then laughed and laughed you did not put that there for my benefit did you. No said my mother Linda the Night Sage, and stop interrupting Now where was I, yes back to the War of the Clans not all of the four clans wished to fight, but what other choice did they have but to fight back, or be captured and killed. Someone had to try to end the war before it was too late; somehow peace had to come to the lands. The fighting went on for far too many cycles and it had to end, for too many people of the clans have died over what? We are a proud people at the end of the cycle's day; we could hold our head high for we worked from solar up to lunar down. What happened to us? Willing to kill one's neighbor, for what a bad look, a wrong word, a dreadful day, is this we have come to? Thousands of shifters had died already, and no end of the war was in sight, blood stained the lands that once held crops and that fed the clans, now it lays baron with nothing but dust blowing. The livestock was left unattended and most died from lack of food and water, they were also killed because shifters and cattle can look alike.

It came to the point that you could not go outside of the Forest for if you did you risked being attacked from all sides. Of course, being in the Forest Clan we could only turn into animals of the forest and as with the other Clans one was of the Water, one of the Air, and the last one of the Desert. Each are limited to its domain, so no Clan could infiltrate an others Clan by the guise of a shifter and invade another's clan threw centrifuge. All the Clan's started equal in every way or so they thought, for when the first clan took to flight to kill its neighboring clan- all bets were off.

Shifting had been natural since the beginning of our cycles, but to use it to kill was unheard of, beyond what all that every clan believed in since birth. How could some shifter due this act of utter dismay, and cruelty, has the world truly turned on its axis? Is this truly the end of all that we know, it cannot be for we believe in the Forest God and he has not called us to his Throne. The Air was hot with the death of the shifters that were attacked and killed .Their deaths now heavy on their minds, Up went screams and cries for the lost, and for the heads of the ones that did this unheard of act that changed our lives in the worse possible way. Now that someone had done the unthinkable it was no longer taboo, and so the turn of the War was a tidal wave of destruction and anarchy. A man killing another man was not a new thing of the past but with all the restrictions lifted all kinds of mythical and fanciful creatures started to show up as though the gates of the Fallen One had been ripped unmercifully off their hinges and thrown shamelessly to the ground. It was not a time of honor or chivalry on the battlefield for one was just trying to keep from being torn to pieces. The old kill or be killed method was now in effect for several of the clans: the main decision that they had to decide was if they also were going to break all the rules. And become something that they could not control, become mindless beasts, puppets for the Dark Lord, or rise and take the high road and fight for what is Just and Right. The Four Clan's we are no more! For even thou the war was far from being over the damage that was done.

The Forest people have always been the healers of the forests and did not know of anything about killing or of war. They prayed to their God "the Great God of the Forest" on which they laid up their prayers that he would answer his people in their time of need. Some said that the Forest God hasn't been seen since the Making Day, but my Mom the Forest Sage knows better, for she is in trusted with the papers of the Great Sages of that time period, and of all time since then including when the Forest God was last seen. In the Enchanted papers of the Sages: it tells of how to reach the Forest God, But first you must pass a series of tests to prove you are clean enough to be in his presence and pure enough for his help.

The War had been taking its toll on all the clans, the forest clan is being hit the hardest because of its stance on not killing its brother or sister clan member just because they live in the wrong area.

The Forest clan was not all alone in the war, for they took in any clan member that was hurt, no matter what their affiliation was in the war.

The only thing that the Forest clan asked before they treated you, was that you did not turn around and attack them, and for some weird reason they never did (must have been something in the medicine.) Some that were healed decided to stay and fight for the services that they received, and others did so out of pride; everyone loves the underdog. So, we are "the underdogs" so what! at least we are still alive, with the people willing to fight for us we have enough to hold off a large attack, but not more than two or three times like that. We still needed a Champion to pass all the tests so our God will come to our aid in this war, the war that may just destroy all the clans if something is not done to bring it to a peaceful end. We put out the word that we needed a Champion that was of pure at heart to take on a series of tests so we can call on our God of the Forest to bring an end to this war. This war has already cost so much death all over the plain; it is all you see is death.

Back in the present time Daphne is still going to school and she only has one year left before she can graduate, and yes, she is still having problems with her History class. She is having a blast in shifting class, she finally got to shift into larger things like Pigs, Donkeys, a Deer but nothing too dangerous for our teacher did want us getting out of control.

You see as you shift into one of the animals, let us say a Bear; you become that animal, as well as yourself. If you are not powerful enough mentally you could be taken over by the animal that you shifted into and become that animal trapped inside it not able to release the hold it has on you.

We put the search for a "Champion" in the faithful hands of our Forest Sage: Williameena the Fire Tamer she dealt with matters of this need. And knew how important that this assignment was and how to bring it to its end.

She started to interview Clan members that thought that they had what it took to be the "Forest Champion," until they found out what the requirements were and most seemed to change their minds very quickly. Some even ran from the tent that was being used for the search of "The Champion," you must understand that part of the testing is a mind probe. Some people do not like what the Sage pulls out of the deepest parts of their minds while looking for qualities of a Champion. If they can handle the mind probe without their brain turning into pulp and running out of their ears, then they can go to Stage Two of the testing. The next Stage of the testing is of the body, to see how much pain that the person could handle before they screamed so loud you would think they were being pulled apart for their write to be the Champion. The right person must be able to endure great pain, all the while keeping under control to be able to think on his/her feet so that they are not killed, because they could not act when it was necessary. These tests that the Sage is putting all the testers threw are nothing compared to the actual Tests of the Forest God may put them thru, which is why they must be so careful to pick the One Pure Champion to go forth and represent the Forest People in their only hope to end the War.

After several more grueling tests most at this point have given up in one fashion or another. The last test is to climb to the top of Mount Blight and find the firebird's nest, overtake it, and bring back one of its eggs. I forgot to tell you the eggs of the Firebird are over 300 degrees and you will have to find a way to bring it back without it burning a hole in your leathers or your skin. Other than that, it should be easy, climb up the side of a burning volcano, plucking an egg from a Firebird while trying not to get burned, race down with the egg no problem. Should not take long you will be done before lunch, dinner if you take your time.

No one returned from the mountain challenge, the Firebirds eat well that day.

With no more challengers for the test, Willimaena called all her clan sisters and went back to her tent to pray what to do next. Now that they have more than one problem, not just a God that is hard to call in a time of need but now the sky is darkening a calling of the Dark Lord is breaking free from his chains. The latest problem is that the sky is getting a darker haze of gray that over the time of the war it seems to be growing in darkness.

Not from the Winter equinox where the days naturally grow darker red, but from what seems to be of a sense of evil taking over that grows and grows stronger the longer the Clans were at War. The Clan's War lasted a Thousand solar years, but the fighting could never last that long could it? Without the "Old Limitations" that were put on them so the Clan's picked new Clan names to stand for their new roles in the War. The Desert Clan is now "Marthlorth's Bloody Raiders" the Sky Clan is now known as: "Garth pan's Plane Riders" and the Sea Clan "Nefrey's Wave Runners. Each of the prefects of the Clan was taken from a great leader in the early years of The Clan Wars. What some call brutal, savage killers, others call their leaders and formed their Clans around them even using their names to bolster their troops. In the start of the war if one killed another person, they would lose their powers FOREVER no exceptions, so needless to say one had to be careful who killed and how. If you planed on keeping your powers you had to have a way or plan to do such a thing. If you killed once, it did not matter you would never get your powers back. This fact for some was hard to live within the starting time of the war. We lived for a long time with our powers, without them. No one knew it could be days or years no one knew for sure only time will tell. After a while there were soldiers upon top of foot soldiers, and they needed a new way to kill now that they were without their powers.

The new weapons did not just pop up, at first, they were very rudimentary sticks, rocks, and things of that sort until some people become fluent with the workings of iron.

They would be able to make all kinds of weapons, but the ore that they needed was across enemy lines, and they did not feel up to asking for it. This went on in the War a lot, if you needed something you could bet that your enemy across the canyon, or over the ridge, or in the pond would have it. You would be playing cosmic chess before you knew it, and the worse part you did not know how to play. As the War wore on the rules of the "Game" got clearer to all in the playing field, for each rule you broke you paid ten cycles in retribution. Like for example: kill someone you lose your shifting powers, and you could die anytime yourself were as if you did not kill you lived for a long time with your powers. So, as you see the Thousand Year War could be fought many ways, if you are the Forest clan you would try not to break any of the rules.

Because they pray to their God of the Forest and need to find someone pure to be their Champion to wake the Forest God so he can end the War. The longer the plains of this red liquid planet are under attack through this War of the Clans there stands a chance of tearing a hole in the lands known as Wardar. Back to the making of weapons once the iron was fought for or (traded for) not so much, it would be melted down to separate the minerals from the ore. All of which is now great for swords, daggers, and things of that nature.

Of course, this is far better than the sticks and stones, but as the War goes on Marthlorth's Bloody Raiders wanted better weapons from their smithies and they were needed to produce newer and better weapons.

Not to be out done the other two fighting Clans wanted the same for themselves, so you could say there was a lull in the fighting for all sides were working on their new weapons of destruction. This as you can see, could be remarkably interesting over the years that went on for they found out that it was important to have people that still had their powers, for they had not killed anyone. This is how the High archery of the clans came into effect; the ones that still had their powers were highly sought after.

Over time the Clans that still had powers were finding new ways to affect the way the War of the Clans was to be played out. New weapons came into the War that had special abilities the Clans learned to cast on the weapons to give them an advantage over the other Clans. Because of these abilities that were formed over time each of the Clans were able to affect the war with this new type of weapon that was being called

"Magic," and the ones that cast this "Magic" were being called Magicians. The Magicians were still bound by the same laws of old; that they could not use their Magic to kill or they would lose their powers.

So, the discovery of the loophole in the old laws they can cast their Magic onto objects to give them magical powers. For example, if you wanted to fill your sword with the magic you could request a meeting with a magician and for the right price, or for a favor they would grant your wish.

Wars were expensive both in gold, and to buy supplies and other goods and in the loss of warrior's lives for in one battle so many lost their lives. Special weapons that had magic cast on to them saved so many lives, depending on which side of the weapon you were on. As the war pressed on both sides were finding it harder and harder to gain an advantage for their magic users both had many skills depending on what clan they were allied to.

As you know from the start, of this retelling each of the four clans had abilities according to their place on this plain. They are known in the old tongue as the Forest Clan, the Sky Clan, The Sea clan, and the Desert clan.(Now the names have changed) but they are still only able to use the ability that Clan names suggests.

The names have changed but still only can control the area of their origins. The Sea clan has abilities from the sea of Water; The Forest Clan has more powers in their protected Forests of their people, and the rest along the same lines. Each Clan was close to being the same in the power of the Magician on each side, but due to the nature of their magic the War was as bloody as ever. If things went on at this rate the War would not end until everyone on all sides was killed, for their hatred for each other would never end. The Forest Clan was the only ones looking for an end to the war that would kill them all if something were not done soon. It was as thou an evil was let loose on the clans that wanted them to kill each other to the very last one. But why was the Forest Clan not affected by the evil that possessed the other Clans. Could it be the Forest and the Magic it held kept them all safe? No one knew for sure, but they were not going to leave the forest to find out. If only they had a Champion to fight for them and pass the tests laid out by their God. Then and only then would the Clans finally have the peace they all needed to end the war and save their way of life. At this point Daphne's Mother said that is enough History for one day. No matter how much she wanted to hear the rest of her mother's history lesson, she knew she would have to wait for their next lesson.

CHAPTER II

Daphne's mother cut off her telling of the history lesson on the Thousand Year War so abruptly she would say that her mother did it on purpose. Any way when her mother said it was time to end, that there is no changing her mind, so you just learn to mind her wishes and go on. Daphne had lost track of time during her mother's telling of their history that she did not realize how late it was. She had a long day at shifting school and could not afford to be late anymore, so off she went to bed with dreams of the thousand-year war in her dreams. It was late when her mother ran to her room for, she heard her daughter scream loud enough for her to think they were under attack of some kind and wake the forest Guard. She had never heard her daughter cry out in such a way before it must be very grave a thing, she thought she would find when she opened the door. That she was relieved to see no one else in the room but her very scared child, and by the look on her face this was no dream. For some time, Linda the Night Sage and Daphne's mother knew her daughter was of the age to see "Visions" but not to the liking of this power. This night would be never forgotten for the Dark Lord must be breaking free of the prison that the Forest God put his in after overpowered him. The great God of the Forest built the prison that he is now trying to break out of. There could be no other reason for a future Sage to cry out in that manner, Linda tried to calm her daughter even though in her heart she knew peace would be lost if they didn't do a Sage linking of her mind to find out how bad it really was. The Night Sage Linda knew she must wake the other Sage if they were not awake and already on their way to hear the calling. But not from her, but her not yet Sage daughter. After trying to calm her coming of age daughter the future Night Sage, that by all things seen after this night on she would grow even more powerful than even her. If this vision is what she thinks it is, there once quiet life would not stay that way for long.

If they did not do something to stop the Dark Lord from escaping from a prison that only another God could escape from. Hopefully, they could somehow slow down the Dark Lord long enough for Daphne to come of age so she can be taught the knowledge of the Sage and hopefully she can learn to control her powers. Poor child I am here, she could hear her mother saying everything will be all right, but both knew it would not.

Both knew that there would be no sleep for either of them for some night to come, the Sage was called, and Daphne now quieter was led to one of the rooms reserved for the council and the Sage if the need arose. And all would soon enough find out what her vision held and how bad the news was that it was given threw a child that is not even a Sage. Yes, she is the daughter of the Night Sage but no that knew of the trouble that Daphne had caused over the years thought this could be possible. All in the Forest would agree that Daphne's life would not be the same from this day forth, there was such a buzz going thru the Forest. First from the shrieking cry and then from the Sage all being brought to the house of the Night Sage in the middle of the night and seeing Daphne hauled off to the council chambers. Anyone that knew the troublemaker of a daughter of the Night Sage thought what has that child done now, but her loyal friends knew there was more to it than that. Daphne being hauled off was not new, by no means and knew she must have gone over the edge this time. The Sage knew only that the child of the Night Sage had done something good this time, for they did not yet hear of the vision and the Dark times for the Forest people and the entire world that they loved so. Many of the people of their quiet had been woke by all the noise and some even taken by the sage and some of the young shifter's that Daphne knew from school were in the council rooms all looking at her. Sitting in a chair wondering what was going only one person they knew of was going to tell them anything. That was the Night Sage and they all knew that they would have to wait for the Sage business to be over.

Before they could find out what was going on, and how Daphne fit into all this mess. Daphne was told to wait in a room and to tell no one of what she saw until the Sage and the Council could find out everything, she saw in her "Vision." Entering the room, she was expecting it to be empty, but it was not there in middle of the room sat her friend Tree Mender, she was so glad to see him. She did not even wonder why he was brought here, if she had she would have known that her mother sent for him to keep her calm, and for company until they could call for her. Daphne did not care why he was there she was scared and was thankful for her friend being there, Tree mender asked how she was doing? And knew he would find out soon enough what happened that night. He also knew he was brought here at this time to solely keep Daphne safe from anyone trying to pry out any information out of her.

And for as to why she screamed so loud it woke up the whole Forest and created such a stir that all the Sage had to be waked up. All Tree Mender was told to do is to keep her company and to keep her safe until there called for her. The latter part had him a little scared, why would she need to be kept safe? He needed to watch his friend closely, until the time someone found it necessary to tell him what was going on. The Night Sage called everyone together in such a hurry that only Daphne and her mother still knew why they were all there. With her daughter safe in another room with Tree Mender she could address to this business, after taking a mental tally of who was present, she knew that everyone was there for her meeting. Being the Night Sage was never an easy job, but it was her calling, and it would not get easy any time soon. So, without any fan fair she told everyone present in the room what she expected from them and what they would have to do to daughter. The Sage melding of minds would not be easy on her daughter. So, she wanted only the strongest Sage to do it so Daphne would not be harmed.

She knew there was no other way to get all the vision to be brought out of her without injuring her, so she made her plans carefully and then she would be called to them. She did not know what happened during her daughter's "vision," but they could not wait any longer, so she called for her right of way. Tree Mender could escort his friend into the room they said for his to bring her to and was surprised by all the people in the room it must have held half the Forest. He was led to a corner while Daphne was taken up to the middle of the room, where she found her mother waiting for her with a look of pride in her eyes, but only she saw the worry in those eyes as well. The Night Sage told everyone why they were there and what she planned to do, there were murmurs in the room than with one look the room went quiet. Walk forward my child was the only words said to her, and she knew that it was time to grow up and walk over to her mother. She and her mother looked into each other's eyes and she knew it was going to be all right. In a booming voice the room new that they were going to try something that was only done in times of great pearl, what had this child seen that is so grave the Night Sage would put her own daughter in great harm. The Sage all started to pray to the God of the Forest to protect the one the he handpicked to tell this vision to and to bring forth the one with his vision. With that Daphne was circled by Sage all praying over her that was when the vision she had in her dream flooded into her mind. She started to scream again for the vision scared her so, but then she could feel the Sage in her mind calming her. Her mother was in her mind also was every one of the Sage, they all saw what she saw and why it frightened her so. All in the room went to their knees weeping for they understood what the vision was, a call to War. A War that would only end with the death of a God, please "let it be the Dark Lord and not their God of the Forest" was all Daphne could think of. After the telling of the vision her secret was out, so why did she not feel relieved?

She began to feel someone's arms around her, she looked up to see her mother wrapping her arms around her and then there was peace. Daphne needed what her mother gave her and was so very thankful for it, for she was able to hold back something that no one could find out yet. Not until it was closer to the time in her vision when she could let everyone know the truth and what part she would be in of: what can only be called "the War of the Gods." Linda Night Sage took her daughter in her arms and walked her to a room with just them for a moment, do not worry I will not tell about your secret just yet. You mean you know about that? She said not to worry, it was between us two, and that no one else knew. Of course, I know about it I am your mother "The Night Sage," she looked down at her daughter with eyes of love and fear, for what she kept from her daughter. For during the reading, she saw something in her vision, that in her fear that even Daphne missed, that would cause her death and Daphne's as well. But that is the future, and we must get her ready for the War, the war that she could lose her daughter, and she dare not tell her for it is the will of the Gods. Will the will of the God's drive her to turn her back on them and everything she believes in, only the God's know? It was early in the day when Daphne could return home to get some much-needed sleep, for not getting much the night before with her vivid vision and the whole Sage thing just drained her. She could sleep if she needed to for her body underwent such a draining process it would be days before she felt normal again. When she woke it seemed like she slept for a fourth night, she opened her eyes and looked around and to her surprise she was not alone. Her eyes took a minute to focus and when they did, she was surprised to see her old friend Tree Mender.

Where you here the whole time I slept? And how long was I asleep? Tree Mender was sent to her room in the morning and it was now time she ate something for she did sleep a fourth night and then some.

Daphne was starving, but what do you expect when you sleep for more than four day and not eat anything.

Boy was she famished and with a not much more of a nod Tree Mender had a minor Sage bring her a large plate of food. The food arrived faster than she would have liked for she wanted to ask her friend some questions, but the Sage returned far too soon. When they brought her meal there was a note from her mother saying,

"We will talk later but for now enjoy our meal and if you want more that will be ok." Daphne devoured everything on her plate and even cleaned the plate so well there was not a crumb left. You must have been starving for I have never seen you eat that much so fast before Tree Mender laughed for it was some site to watch. She apologized about her manors and then let them take the plate, so she could talk to her friend alone. So, what do you want to talk about first? The fact that the forest was buzzing about you and the Sages. There are so many rumors that your head would spin right off, how about you were taken by the Sage for your outburst in the night and kept in the dungeons. Or how about that you must have used your shifting powers again and there was whew knows what flying around and the sage were called to banish the creature. That you must of cast to get out of your chores again, and that is why you were not in Shifting School all week. Daphne was not shocked by all the rumors, but she was scared about Shifting School and what they were told about her absence. That would have to wait until she was able to talk to her mother the Night Sage and find out what she told her school. She prayed to the Forest God that she would not get kicked out of shifting school not with things going so well. Her mind was a little foggy and Tree Mender was told she would be at first than after a while it would come flooding back.

Daphne was not looking forward to that for everything was so vivid it seemed so real like she was experiencing it firsthand, and that truly scared her the most.

She was not ready for the War to come and did not know how much time they all had to prepare for the coming of the Dark Lord. They still had time to stop him from breaking out the prison that only a God could build. She had to talk to her mother soon but knew her mother would be working to see her Vision to find out the answers that they all needed to find out. She so wanted things to be back to a time before her Vision, and the life that she now knew she would never see again. If they could stop the Dark Lord from breaking his bonds it was not too late. After talking to Tree Mender for a while she was more frustrated than ever, for he was not allowed to talk about anything from that night. She hoped that her mother was able to be available to see her soon, for she had so many questions.

She very much needed a hug from her mother, not the Night Sage just her mother to calm her fears. If she could just forget about everything to do with that dumb Vision and everyone it would affect. She talked to Tree Mender for a long time, until to her surprise her mother was standing at the door of her room with a big smile. The mother that she knew as a child was looking at her with pride, she needed it to last longer but new it would not for, above all her mother was the Night Sage and there would be many long nights before she saw that look again. Her mother started to tell her about what had been happening in the Forest when she was recovering from the process, they used on her, and that is when it happened. Daphne was hearing her mother's voice not with her ears but in her mind, she heard her mother so clear she could not believe what was happening to her. The look on her face must have been quite precious that was when the Night Sage spoke to her and said that "no she was not going bonkers." She went on to say that it was part of the outcome of the Linking and the connection she would have with her mother the Sage.

Daphne was now freaking out that she yelled that you can now read my mind of something, how long will that last. Calmly mother Sage told her daughter to keep her voice down that these were secrets of the Sage and no one could find out.

And no, I cannot read your mind, but I can talk to you now with my mind and you can do as so with me and no other. It is part of the Linking process that the Sage in charge of the Linking keeps a link with the one that they read their Visions from; in this case it was your mother. As for as how long it lasts it is permanent if you live, but let us talk of other things, like your acceptance into the Sage and tomorrow will be your first day, after shifting school. You mean I can still go? That is great she can still see all her friends that must be worried sick about her. What do we do now? Wait a minute did you say "That I was going to be a Sage like you" wow was it because of what happened? Would I be in Sage School if I did not have a Vision of our doom? No that was not even considered when the vote came up, it was because you were ready, and the Vision proved that.

You are destined to be a Great Sage more powerful than even your mother, so it is late, and you have a long day tomorrow with classes and all.

Do not worry about your absence from your classes it is all taken care of we covered up what happened that night. You were reported to be gravely ill and that is your cover story you were bitten by a poisonous spider and that was why everyone was running around trying to find a way to stop the poison and save your life. You are not to tell anyone about the Vision and what really happened or that you are now in Sage training. After all that happened in the last several days it was hard to just act like nothing happened at Shifting School, and all the questions of what happened and are you ok? Did it hurt after you were poisoned? All great questions if that were how things went the last fourth night when I saw the Vision that would change all our lives. I just wanted to stop telling all the lies that I had to tell at school to my friends and my teachers, but I will say one thing about the cover story.

When the Sage lies about something, they make it so convincing that even with the truth in front of you, everyone wants to believe the lies. For the Sage were so revered, people were compelled to believe anything they said and not to question them or what they say.

After lying all day to everyone it was nice when Tree Mender came to school to join me for lunch. I knew he was sent by the Sage, but it was the break away from the lies that I needed. To be with some one that I could be myself, Daphne gave her friend a big hug for she was so happy to tell the truth to someone that would believe her because he was also there. Tree mender asked her how she was holding up. And for the first time today Daphne was glad to tell the truth, before the night of the Vision she would not have wanted to tell the truth so much, she was already changing? She did not care at the time she just wanted to talk to her friend without prying eyes to see what she was saying or doing was part of the story. Yes, she was being watched for there are not so many Sages around her any other time, so they must be there to spy on her and make sure she stuck to the story they agreed to.

She would have to talk to her mother later about it but for now she wanted to enjoy her lunch with Tree Mender. He said that he had been requested to take a leave of absence from his work in the forest for as long as the Sage thought it necessary.

He said that he was for a lack of better words her bodyguard and would be there after school to escort her to the first day in Sage training. The bell for lunch rang and Daphne went back to class, to be met by her new bodyguard after she got out for the day. What would Sage training be like, she had thought about it for years, after all her mother was the Night Sage, it was expected for her to follow in her mother's steps. But she always thought it would be after her mother's death not like this.

Even under the circumstances she was excited for it had been all she had dreamed of as a small child watching her mother at work and wondering how it would be.

As expected, Tree Mender was there to escort her to Sage training, she could not wait for she had been thinking about nothing else. So, when she was led to a room with nothing in it, she started to wonder if she was in the right place. Just then she heard her mother's voice in her head, she turned around to greet her and she was not there.

It then dawned on her that the voice she heard was in her mind and not in the room at all. Her mother said that she was going to be her teacher today and she would be late so I was to eat the food that would be brought. Just as she heard in it her mind in came walking Tree Mender who was there to keep her company while her mother was delayed. She did not care that her mother was going to be late for she was famished and after all Tree Mender was there to keep her company. She started in on the food that was brought so nicely by her friend and new bodyguard that she did not even think if he had eaten himself. Would you like anything to eat after all there was plenty, much more than she could eat by herself. He kindly turned her down saying that he had eaten earlier while he was waiting on her to get out of school, he also said that her mother sent extra for according to her Daphne would need it for it was to be a long night.

Daphne finished eating just as she heard the door opening, and someone called for Tree Mender to leave he said he would see her after her class if it was not too late. Just after he left, she heard her mother's voice in her head, saying she was on the way. She could not get use to her mother's voice in her mind, and she made a mental note to ask how it was done.

In walked her mother with two other Sage, she could see a big pile of books held by one of them and hoped that they were not for her.

The other Sage had a table in his hands and set it down next to Daphne to which the books were placed, she saw some of the books in the pile seemed to be incredibly old.

The Sage were excused, and her mother sat on a pillow on the floor next to her daughter, before you freak out by all the books, some are for the entire year and others are just for research. She gave her daughter a big hug and asked how her day went, saying she hoped it went well and not too many questions about her "sickness." If the Sage had done their job well all the questions were already dealt with, she told her mother that everything went well including her new bodyguard.

Now that we have addressed the formalities, we can get on with your Sage training, first she dealt with Daphne and everything to do with the Vision. The Night Sage her mother was concerned with her child and all that went with the whole Vision. She went on to say that she was proud of her and how rare it was for a Sage to be called upon to speak for the God. And how it never happened to a lay person yet alone a child of her age, it has never in their history happened this way.

CHAPTER III

Sage Training

Linda the Night Sage went on to explain how Daphne's Sage training would go ahead, and that She would not be her teacher, but she wanted to be the to explain how the training would go. You will still see me from time to time, but my Sage business would take me away too much to be there for every class. After the hearing of the Vision she had no time with her trying to stop The Dark one from breaking his locks and preventing a War. Your Teacher was picked out with your tendencies to get let say "bored" and you wanting for a better way to do things in mind. You must not think lightly of your training from this day on for you were chosen by the Forest God to deliver his message and you must be prepared to do his work. As a Sage our lives encircle the needs of the people and the wishes of our God, we must be trained in the way to lead the Forest people. From this day your training will be so you can learn the ways of Sage and the secrets that only Sage can hear. Tonight, we are going to learn about the rest of the War of a Thousand Years and how the Dark Lord came to the plane, and what it took to remove him. We have the Forest God to protect us; the others outside of our reach were all affected by which at the time was called the Darkness for that was the way it looked.

The Sky was not as Red, and the swirling affect that you see when you look up was duller than anyone could remember. We did not know that the evil or the Darkness that was seen was due to the hate each Clan had for one another. The longer the War continued the Darker everything got, the sky, the fields and our hearts got, to the point one could stop the Darkness from taking over.

The Forest was spared for we kept out of the War directly and our God still looked down on his people and protected them. It was not until the latter years of the War that even our God lost some of his power due to the influence of the darkness.

That was why we had to find a Champion to go through the trials, and to be tested to the point that nothing but a pure vessel could enter in the Forest God's presence. We searched for over hundreds of years for the Champion to be found, all that time the war raged on, and the Darkness got worse every day. The power of the Dark one was so great it took over the other Clans and they started to worship him as their God, or as they called him the God of War. With the other clans worshiping the Dark One his power over our plane grew, it affected all the Clans even ours. With such an evil power taking over our God went into isolation for the Dark power was so great that the Forest God had to flee the plane so he could have the power to overtake the Dark Lord when the time came. We as his Sage understood his thinking for, we did not blame him for leaving us in the hands of The Dark One. The time would come for him to return and we prayed it would be soon, without him here to fight for us the Darkness covered the land. We needed a Champion more than ever and we had to find the qualified candidate to go before the Forest God and pass his tests for him to return and remove the Darkness from the Land. The Sage were proven after the evil flooded the land with a black darkness that could only be from his people, the other clans praying to their God, not knowing what they released upon not just them but all of us. The Darkness lasted longer than anyone could predict, and with no one sowing the fields, the fields no longer were able to bear it is bounty and people starved.

With no food things got very bleak and that brought the end of the War, that lasted a Thousand years only to come to its end due to no one left alive to fight or was it a God that intervened? The Forest was spared most of the effects of the Darkness brought on by the Dark Lord, for the prayers put up to the God of the forest saved his people from starving and dying off as the others had.

The creatures of the woods still played in it branches and the larger game was present but in declining numbers as the years past. We would surpass to the same fate of the clans of the Dark one hand, if somehow a Champion was found or born. That was the answer and we never thought of it! The only way to find a Champion would be of a pure birth of a Sage, and to raise it a pure child destined to grow up to save his/her people. So, you see Daphne there are no such thing as co-instances, you were chosen now just like a child was chosen then. What Daphne did not know was that her mother was the child that grew to be tested and chosen to save her people. A Sage is chosen at birth and sent to be tested once they reach age, there powers progress until around puberty where her abilities grow to their fullest. At that point they can complete the calling according to their abilities as a young Sage in training. At the end of Sage training they must remain pure and never marry, for threw the pureness of the Sage they intervene for their people and take prayer to the Forest God. The more abilities a Sage has she can be lifted to as far Night Sage, but a Sage is in her called position until they pass on or Can not continue in the service of the Forest God. The Sage with the most powers is the highest and strongest Sage in their order and all respect her for their powers or abilities are believed to be given by the Forest God himself.

Also, a Sage that has more powers is the one that lives the longest of her people, for her powers keep her alive and able to serve their God longer. So, it is not unusual for a sister or Sage to live longer than any other clan member as it is with Daphne's mother the Night Sage. Linda the Night Sage was born right at the end of the Thousand Year War, about sixteen years to be exact.

When she was born no one had yet knew of her potential or her destiny, she was raised by a poor family with no ties to the Sage or to the Forest God. It was not until she reached the age of testing that Linda even had any power, and no one knew of her special abilities.

She was scoped up by the Sage right away when the testing revealed just how well she scored and just how powerful she would soon be.

Linda was put into Sage training early for her abilities were to be the highest that any hopeful Sage of any age.

They were correct about her, for she showed signs of her ability's far sooner than any tested since they started keeping records. She had the best teachers the best cloths the best of everything for she was a prodigy. She had to be conditioned in every way for they knew some day she could do a great many things in the name of the Forest God. No one including Linda the Sage would go on to save the world that they loved so, not even Linda know of the plans the Forest God had in mind for her. She learned about everything a Sage was trained for in half the time, her mind was a wet sponge and soaked up everything put before her. She loved reading and she read so fast; the Sage ran out of books for her to read. So, the decision was made to work on her abilities to keep her busy. Linda knew about everything books could teach her so now she would learn to put it to practical use. Where she also excelled and learned to Shift faster than any other student had. Learning for her was away to explore what she could only see only in her dreams; she could not get enough. A prodigy did not get to do what they wanted and for her to get out and explore was out of the question, so in her mind she would explore the places that she could only dream about. Linda was not given many opportunities to make many friends while she was in Sage training so when she got the chance to talk to an instructor about something the little schoolchild in her craved knowledge as being given a sweet treat. Linda was well liked by all her teachers and each of them had a fondness for her as thou they were her family. This fondness Linda took advantage of for she was desperate to get out from time to time, and if she could get one of her teachers to just break the rules. Then she would ask them to break the rules just this once, and occasionally, she was successful. As she got older, she was able to go out to the forest and forage for food with a guard to watch out for her.

They had a War at the edge of their Forest, and they did not want their prodigy killed before she could save them from the Evil that was taking over everyone outside of the Forest. The hunt for the Champion was something Linda heard of most of her life, for that person was going to be the one to save them from all this dammed War. Linda finished Sage training and now had the freedom to do some of the things she dreamed about, if she finished her assigned duty that is. Being the youngest Sage ever did not bother her in the least, but there was always someone that was jealous of her .As for they were older than her and did not like taking orders from a younger person, or she passed up some others in Sage training and they were mad. Because they thought she got special treatment from her teachers which she did, but they did not see how hard they were on her because she was a prodigy. Linda did get away with some things depending that the teacher of the day was. Her favorite was Sage Mother Clarisse she was a lot older and was like the grandma she never had, she let her get away with the most because she reminded her of her granddaughter. After being a Sage for a period of years Linda became more worried each day about the War, and the power of the Dark One or as his followers called him the Dark Lord. A Champion was still not found and each day that passed the Darkness got blacker and darker as with people's attitudes. It was nothing to see someone fighting with a neighbor or friend over something that neither was sure of why the fight started. The Sage knew that if their God did not step in soon all may be lost, Linda prayed to her God increasingly every day for him to intervene. One night she was dreaming about what the challenges of the Forest God's tests and what it would be like to be the Champion.

Then clear as day the face on the Champion was her face and the Forest God told her "what are you waiting for, you know in your heart you are the Champion that I am looking for."

With that she woke with up and ran down the stairs to where the parchment of the challenger's was for people wanting to be tested to be Champion. She signed her name big and bright Linda the Night Sage, for in her dream this was the title the Forest God gave her as his

Champion. She knew in her heart that she was the only one that could pass all the test's put forth by their God. When the next morning when the sky was not so black people arose from their beds to hear about this new challenger calling herself "The Night Sage." Linda was scared when she heard some of the rumors going around about The Night Sage for, she wanted to break it to the head of the Sage herself. She was worried that they were trying to prevent her from entering the challenge or worse expel her for calling herself by a title not given to her by the Sage. As it seemed she would look at a council of the Sage punishing her if they did not believe her dream and the name the Forest God gave her himself. That afternoon she was called to the head Sage's office Linda knew of her threw her studies but never seen her in person, this was not good she said to herself. Linda was escorted to Gretta the High Sages office and was told to sit down outside of her office and wait for her to call you in. Linda the Night Sage sat outside of the highest Sage office waiting to be called in, while she waited, she prayed to her God to intervene. The door opened and she was asked to sit in front of her desk while she finished some papers that had to get signed right away. Gretta was a lot younger than Linda thought for she did not know that with higher abilities that you age slower so she was shocked when she saw to Sage before here looked to be younger than some of her teachers when she was in Sage training. She must have been staring at her for Gretta said to her "like what you see," with that Linda realized what she had done and apologized to the High Sage before her.

Gretta laughed and said not to worry child for I get those looks all the time, do not you remember about how one's abilities keeps them younger.

Before Linda could say anything, Gretta changed the subject at hand "what is this I hear about you calling yourself The Night Sage?" As this was the name you used on the ledger for the challenge, that is you is it not? Not wanting to upset her Linda started to explain about her dream and how the Forest God himself gave her the name, when she was stopped and told to hold her tongue. The High Sage explained that she did not call her down to be told about some dream that she may or may not of had, I called you down here to find out about that "title" you gave on the roster. Linda the Night Sage is that correct? Slowly Linda explained about how she was given the name and that it meant she would be the one to defeat the Darkness and The Dark One. And bring back the Day by overcoming the Challenges set forth by their God and become his Champion against evil. The High Sage looked back at her with shock in her eyes and with a shaky voice said "you are the face that I saw in my dreams for you are the one we have been looking for to save our people and this miserable plane we all live on. We must waste no time for you are the chosen one, and to think we had you under our noses this whole time. Thank the God of our people for you are here to save us all, we must start your training right away. For being a Sage, you have abilities that will no doubt help you on your journey. We have no time to waste we must call the council together and all the people together to announce that a Champion has been found by the name of Linda the Night Sage. Linda asked Gretta what made you believe me that face could have belonged to anyone why did you believe me? Gretta said, "What only you can have dreams child?" and with that they both laughed aloud.

Now come child we have a lot of work to do, you will it seems be terribly busy from now on I would say. Linda had no idea as to where to start or how to get to the place of her God or as to how to start her quest. Gretta the High Sage was calling for her, all day and night to comb threw some ancient books or map, or legend that was passed down.

For they both were working hard to make her trip safe and successful, Linda also had to ensure that she succeeded both for her life as that of her people. With the help of Gretta and all the other Sage she knew where to start, not a lot more than that, but it was a start. Linda was not one to "wing it" or to go into something without doing her research with not much to go by she would have to do her best and rely on her God to get her threw this. After hearing this story from her own mother, it clicked in her head and she shouted aloud "you were the Champion!" All this time you never told me, that is so cool that my mother help defeat the Dark Lord. The Forest God defeated the Dark One not me child and if you are done with your outburst I will continue. You can ask me questions later, now, where was I? Yes, I remember we were about to get to the best part, right before you interfered with your outburst. Daphne apologized to her mother and asked her to continue, but man she had so many questions for later. Her mother left off with the one thing that all their research gave them was a place to start, it was high up on the volcano at the end of their plane called "death creator." Death Creator was more than inhospitable for it was a volcano that she would have to climb down into its depths to start her journey with no one to help her once the quest had started. Linda the Sage could take as much supply as she could carry but nothing more, and no one to talk to all those dark and dangerous nights ahead.

The Creator that she had to climb down was no place for a Sage yet alone for a woman. Thank the Forest God that she was given this mission to save the world and her friends, and even the ones that did not deserve to be saved. It was decided that the night of her departure the Forest people would have a huge dinner in her honor, but due to the War around them they did not want to draw attention to her. In the event someone would make it their goal to stop her for the Dark one would never allow her to defeat him. So, without any fanfare of any kind it was decided she should leave that night and that she would be careful to travel with one guard.

To see her threw out the Bad Lands so as not to be killed before being able to start her challenge. With some words of encouragement Linda was set for her trip to the Volcano but first she was introduced to her guide. She learned that he had lots of experience outside the forest and was protecting its people since the start of the Clan Wars and was gifted in the art of warfare. Linda the Night Sage, this is Beaver Tail as he is called in the Forest, elsewhere you may hear other names that he has been called by, but he prefers Beaver Tail. How do you do? I am fine. It would be best if we discuss the best way to travel to Death Creator where I will wait for you for four days if you do not return I will presume you are dead and will return to the Forest. Unless our God tells me to wait then I will wait only long enough for what is safe then I will be forced to fall back to a safer place to wait. I am at your service, but I ask you to follow and do as I say until the time for your challenge. We don't want to lose the best chance we have to get out of this terrible Thousand Year War it would be best that we go in our current forms even thou shifting would be more convenient it would also make us stand out for there are not many Forest creatures where we are going.

Linda the Night Sage agreed to his terms and on they went out of the safety of the woods she knew and out in the evil that was taking over their plane. In the Forest they are protected from the Dark One and his powers, but Linda was not ready for the on slot of his powers as soon as they stepped out of the forest.

She almost fell over from its pushing on her that she had to brace herself in what must have looked as thou she fell or stumbled. Beaver Tail saw what she tried to hide not so well and said should of warned you of that, do not worry it hits everyone the same if they had never felt it due to the protection of the forest. Beaver Tooth said to Linda the Night Sage you can call me "Beaver" if you wish all my friends do, and some that are not my friends. Beaver how long do you think it will take to get to the creator?

I do not know we may have to stop, due to many things on the way, and I may have to fight off defenders of the Dark One and kill some of them. Linda was shocked to her core at how he said "he might have to kill some of them" she would never kill someone for she would lose her powers to Shift. She asked "have you killed someone before" I don't want you to lose your powers over me, he saw the worried look in her eyes and lied by saying "do not worry I lost my powers in the early years of the war". He did not want her to worry about that now and that is why he lied, but he knew he would kill in a heartbeat to safe the only hope they had. It is late and you have shifting school in the morning young lady, and do I have to tell you not to say anything about any of this going on.

Off to bed and Tree Mender will be waiting to escort you tomorrow and will see you home, if anyone asks you why Tree Mender is walking you around change the subject. We of course will have to produce a better story as to his affection over you lately, you could help with that. Now go to bed child for I here you have a surprise test in shifting 101, hope you studied. Daphne was awakened early by a bad dream and went to find something to take her mind off her dream, in the kitchen Daphne ran into the last person she wanted to see, the hall guard. Since her vision and her enrolling in Sage training her things were moved to the Sage main dormitory, where at night is all a little spooky. Miss Daphne why are you not in your room asleep, is everything ok? Can I help you with something so you can return to your room? Daphne forgot that the halls of the dorms where watched by Freshman Sage and of course that meant no walks to the kitchen without getting caught.

I am sorry I needed some water and I did not think anyone would mind if I helped myself. As you see it is way pass kitchen hours so if you need some water it will be brought to your room before you retire from now, so you do not get caught wondering around past curfew again. Thank you that would be lovely, I will go back to my room so I can get back to sleep.

May I take a glass of water with me just for tonight?

Of course, if you do not get in trouble for helping me escape from my bad dreams. Thanks again I must go I am told that there is a test that I must pass tomorrow so if I can get my water I will go? Here you go since you are new, I guess we can cut you one brake; just do not tell anyone where you got it. The birds that chirped outside of Daphne's window woke her with a sleepy desire to skip school and sleep in, but of course she would no longer be able to get away with sleeping in. Just as if on cue there was a knock on the door announced that breakfast was now being served. Daphne was told that she was behind schedule and that there would be no time to eat her meal if she did not hurry. Daphne got dressed and wolfed down her breakfast for as she was told she was running late.

There was a knock again to announce that Tree Mender was waiting to escort her to shifting school. On the way she asked Tree Mender if he knew about this morning's surprise test. From the laughter coming out of him she knew the answer to her question. Why did you not warn me so I could study? This brought more laughter as well with an elbow to his ribs.

CHAPTER IV

Daphne could not believe all the people at school that wanted to ask her question after question, "Are you ok"? "What happened to you? We heard all the noise, what happened? We heard the scream and then Sage we are running everywhere. She was so overwhelmed by all the attention that she could not wait for school to be over, but first came the test in Shifting 101. That is when Daphne received word from her mother via the new connection they had. The Mind Shifting of the other night left a link that her mother now used to let her know something that she does not want others to hear. Just wanted to ask you how you are doing? I heard about all the attention you received today and wanted to tell you some good news. The test in shifting 101 is an oral test on your Shifting abilities so far, wanted to get you tested in the events that have happened in the last couple of days. It is all stuff you already know, but I wanted to find out how proficient at Shifting so we can do away with the need for the Sage to test you for your new classes. Sorry about not telling you about it sooner, some Sage of a small sect are questioning whether you have the abilities needed to become a sage.

What is it that I picked up about you having bad dreams? Hope you are just having bed dreams and not The Dark Lord manipulating your mind? You may be on his radar now that you had a vision about him breaking loose, if you need me I can check on you to see if you are ok tonight, and if you are on his radar I will be able to see your dreams threw our link. Good luck in our Shifting class I know you will do ok for you are the daughter of the Night Sage. Daphne felt that her mind was hers again and decided that she could not put it off any further so off to her Shifting class she went.

The testing was harder than she thought it would be thanked god she did not shift anything out of nature like "A long nose Bear bat" like she did years ago. She could not believe that it had been so long ago since that day she tried to get out of doing some choirs. I guess I did better than I did that night at least, hopefully a lot better for it seemed by her dreams that she would need all the help she could get. Her mother was right about being on the Dark Lords radar and he was not happy about all his plans to break the bonds of his prison, to be foiled by a mere child.

Daphne's nightmares were coming increasingly as time grew shorter as his hold on this world increased. If a child not yet a Sage could see the Dark Ones plans for this world surely others with greater powers than hers could also. This fact alone scared Daphne into doing the one thing she dreaded, telling her mother and if she knew her Mother Daphne was about to lose any freedom she had left. As she thought when she told her mother about her nightmares the first thing, she did was to order someone to watch over her around the clock. That was the thing that she prized most was now gone from now to who knows how long no more sneaking out for her. With Tree Mender watching her during the day light hours and now the Sage watching her at night at least if she had visits by the Dark Lord in her sleeping hours someone would be there with her.

Only her mother could predict the role that Daphne had in all this mess in stopping the Dark Ones plans to conquer their world. This time it would take more than just her, for it would require her daughter as well. Daphne was informed that her mother was to be teaching her lessons for Sage training from this point in her training. After shifting school Tree Mender was there to escort her to Sage Training with her mother. Now she could hear more about how her mother Linda the Sage became the Night Sage and her quest to find the Forest God.

Daphne was taken to the classroom where her lessons took place, only to find a note from her mother telling for her to meet in her mother's office.

As if on cue Tree Mender was there to escort her to the offices of the High Sage, where her mother had asked her to meet her. She expected to find her mother alone, but when she was led into the office, she saw they were not alone. Gretta the High Sage was in the room as well, this made Daphne worried that she was in some way in trouble with seeing Gretta, of all the Sage to have a meeting with. She was about to apologize thinking she could not be in the right room until her mother called to her to come in and shut the door. Of course, Daphne had heard of the high Sage Gretta and never thought that she would be to in the same room with the High Sage and not being chastised for a monument of bad judgment. That is when her mother informed her, she was to be taught by Gretta as well for the next couple of lessons; this is when Daphne thought she would pass out of shock. Linda, her mother, and Gretta the High Sage where friends for over a thousand cycles. As you may remember from the stories that I told you since birth, I was the one that passed the Forest Gods trials and was proven worthy to enter his inner chambers. The Forest God was amazed upon seeing me for the first time, but the thing that impressed him the most was my early age. For at the time I was but a young child by his standers, I was not even 100 years old when I became the Champion. He commented on it, and the grave state that the world must be in if the only one of his people worthy was a child, but she did pass all his tests so she must be special indeed.

The Forest God asked her "what do they call you child" Linda felt the power that came from him and answered him with all the power that she could muster.

They call me "Linda the Night Sage" and Champion for your people, for I am the one that saw the Dark Lord breaking out of his prison that you yourself put him in.

Yes, I also felt a shift in the balance of power, but up to this time I had hoped that I was wrong and that the Dark one was safely packed away in the prison. Tell me child what did you see in your vision. I recanted the vision that showed the Dark Lord removing the seals of his confinement. I informed his of the details of my dream and wanted to tell him that my name was "Linda the Night Sage" not child. But I thought better of it after all his is our God and if he wants to call me "child" then so be it, for I did not come here to worry about my pride. For the nightmares that she was having were visions of what would happen if she failed in her mission to request the help of their God, the God of the Forest. My Lord I appeal you to help all our lands before the Dark Lords hold get any stronger, for as it is the black cloud that covers most of our lands grows darker with each passing day. Fear not Linda of the Sage for I am more powerful than that weasel that you call the Dark One and with my plans for him, he will wish he never threatened my people. I will request your aid in this matter for your link with the Dark Lord may come handy in dealing with him. Linda was overwhelmed with pride for the Forest God wanted her help defeating the Dark One. Yes of course I will aid you in this mission to save the world it would be my honor, I am all ways your servant, how could she say no to a God. Let us be real does a God care if you must do your homework and that is why you could not help him. It is my duty as a Sage to offer my services in any way possible.

"Sage" you need not to hesitate in your heart or mind for it could be extremely dangerous for you to do so, your strength need not hesitate one bit or you could perish. Linda knew in her heart that someday she might have to give her life for her beliefs let us just hope it would not be soon.

Daphne was so shocked by the ease of the telling from her mother and had to interfere long enough to find out some key things that her mother left out. Mother I do not understand something from the telling of your time with The Forest God, what kind of trials were there? And how did you know what to do?

First child you do not interrupt me when I am telling of our history for the things that I leave out at this time, I will come back to it another time.

Right now, I want you to absorb as much as you can, ok? Now, where was I? Yes, I remember I was about to go help The Forest God save the world. But your questions do have merit so I will go back a way so you can understand everything, ok? Daphne was upset about her mother punishing her for not waiting, but she had to find out everything because in her heart she knew it may be important to her someday. Ok let us go back to the first time that I stepped out of our Forest and the shock at the sight of plains ahead of me, my Guide was terribly angry with me at first. For you see I had been in the Forest of our lands my whole life and the shock which before me was more than I could handle being so fresh to the destruction and mayhem that I saw everywhere. We only traveled a mere five miles the first couple of days, for my poor feet were blistered from the soft living and being pampered. Beaver Tail my guide was disappointed with the progress we were making and took it upon himself to fix the matter of our poor progress. From now on you will have to push yourself more and after a couple of days the blisters will heal, and you should be able to travel more each day.

The shoes that I had used my whole life I now dreading the choices in travel attire, my poor feet hurt so badly from my soft living. Beaver Tail was right and after about a week of hard travel and a few changes in my attire we made much better time we traveled mostly at night. When we came upon villages, we were extra careful, so no one asked any questions or worse tried to kill us and take the trivial things we had for them.

We took truly little on the trip, not because of the money problems but to attract less attention, incase if anyone wanted to turn us in to The Dark Lord for a reward. If they found what we were up to there would be many a fiend deciding to do just that, so far, the Dark Lord did not know of our trip and we wanted to keep it that way.

We took hard tack and dried bread that was stale after a few days into the trip; we chose to cover the miles by foot so we would not have to explain were we got horses. We did not use any shifting magic so we could stay under the radar of any dark forces, the farther that we traveled we found less friendly faces and more of the kind that wanted to kill you just for the way you looked. The lands outside of our wonderful forest were cold and dark with no friends to be found and many enemies to be had. We talked to no one weather they looked friendly or not so the word would not get out that there was a Champion willing to try to make a change. The Dark One could not know of our progress for the fear that we would put out the word that we needed to be stopped. We traveled better farther away from anyone at night so no one would know we were even there. The Food ran out first and we had to find food anyway we could without jeopardizing our chances of passing the trials, there was little food left anywhere and the ones with it did not let go of it cheap. There was a many a day that we went without food and were just lucky enough to find fresh water, in the streams that were left there was no fish. We prayed to the God of our people and he supplied what we needed and the protection from any enemies. The Days became the worse for we could not travel and there was little food, so we sat around a small fire so as not to draw attention. Beaver Tail was on watch while I slept so we are not surprised, and I did the same for him while he slept.

Over time he became less angry with me and we talked about the days when the Darkness would be gone, and the lands could return to their earlier glory.

I found that over time we became friends and he taught me many of the things he used to survive in this God forsaken land, the fondness that I felt was returned to me by the man that would become your father!

What? Why had you not told me of this sooner and if you had to stay pure how could he be my father? That is a story for another time but know this after we brought piece back to the land, we were able to mate and find love. So, then Beaver Tail is my father Daphne said? What happened to him? Is he still alive? No child he died shortly after we made it back.

Now no more questions on this matter, for I will tell you everything another time. Ah yes now back to the telling we traveled well together, and we made up lost time. My visions were getting stronger by the day, He was growing in power and soon he will be able to feel my abilities and the plan that we are trying to stop him. The journey to the crater of the Forest God was very well guarded, and we had to travel across many barren lands affected by the blight that was brought forth by a Demy- God. One of which did not want to be locked up and was doing everything in his power to get out, and one could feel the effects on the plain. We ran into some trouble along the way by a group of the Dark one's followers that stumbled upon us by chance, Beaver tail dispatched them without too much problem. This was but an attack on anyone that walked into their property and thank fully they had no clue who we were. But eventually the Dark One will have enough of a hold in this plain that he will be able to send out Dark troupes under his control to stop us. With the encounter Beaver Tail decided that it was time for me to learn to defend myself in the event he should become overpowered. He knew of my vows to stay pure to the Forest God and that I needed to stay that way, as he said, "what good is it if I perish before I get there."

If I just defended myself long enough to escape from a would-be attacker, that way I would not break my vows, and lose my powers in the same instance.

We had to be more careful than ever for we were about to enter the

darkest and most hostile part of our trip and my training in self-defense was more important than ever. The times where we were not traveling, it was all lessons after lessons. Beaver Tail pushed me hard for he could see the natural ability in me. We trained as thou I was in the fiercest battle each time when I picked up a dagger or a sword there was no holding back. Each new lesson of war faire was so drilled into me so that it was instinct, for this way I would react and not stumble in battle, or just a friendly dull with swords. I had a great teacher who taught me to defend myself, and he saw a bright student that could overcome any thing put before her. Along the way we ran into more desperate people that were trapped in the web of the Dark one is doing. And of course, the highway men that attacked anything or anyone that they met, and then there was the mercenary that served the Dark forces and did his bidding. Most of the people of our plain knew some dark force was at work and its effect was changing our world into a dark and fore bidding place that in time only evil could live in. Some prayed to their God's for help but the help they requested fell on deaf ears, for even the God's of the people were not powerful enough to stop the Dark one's work. The only hope we had in saving our land we put in the lap of Linda the Night Sage. With those words Daphne was informed that would be the end of the telling for the night and Tree Mender escorted her to her rooms for the night. Daphne said good night to Tree Mender and got ready for bed, but what she did not know was that her dreams would be the darkest of all. For her mother may have been able to stop the Dark forces of her day, but this time there would be no stopping him. Not while he lived, he would not go back into his dungeon, for he would die first. Daphne was screaming and covered with sweat when her mother ran into her room to wake her poor daughter.

No matter what Linda did she could not wake Daphne from the evil that had taken over her dreams and possessed her. Linda knew of only one way to bring her child back from the evil grip that prevented Daphne from awaking, a mind-link with her could work to bring her out of the grip the Dark one had on her. But there was no time to gather the Sage Council she must act fast or Daphne may not come out of his hold.

Linda had never tried a linking without the Sage to keep her safe and bring her back if necessary. She had no one close enough to help with the mind-linking due to the hour of the night; all she could hope for was Tree Mender hearing the screaming and run to wake the Sage. Hopefully in time to bring them both back or they could be lost in her mind and in the grip of the Dark Lords power forever. Linda had a link with her daughter already, so it was not hard her to link with Daphne, but she was not ready for what she saw in the trapped mind of her daughter. The evil and dark power in Daphne's mind was so strong that Lind had to fight just to keep the link open to her child. No matter how Linda tried to reach her daughters mind she would find a wall so high she that she could never reach her in time to rescue her without help from her sisters of the Sage. Linda was fighting a losing battle just to stay in her child's mind until reinforcements could arrive. If Linda could not do something soon, she could lose her only child to the Dark Lord, and she would never let that happen if she breathed. The power that she felt in the mind of Daphne shocked her and she was not prepared for the on slot of the evil that she felt. It felt like days even though she knew it was less than an hour when she was pulled back from the brink in Daphne's trapped mind. Linda fell to the floor in a heap and was taken right away to her rooms to recover from the link that nearly trapped her in a mind she no longer recognized as that of her precious child.

When Linda woke in her bed, she did not understand how she got there, but was thankful for her sisters of the Sage that they were able to come to her aid. She called for any one of the Sage in training that would be at her door to help her up, for she was so weak she could not yet get out of bed on her own. That is when the call went out that she had finally awaken and the High Sage was called forth to help her recover from the immense pressure on her mind due to the Dark Lords trap. She asked for her daughter and if she was ok? She received back startled looks which made her scared for Daphne's safety. Where is my child, and why won't anyone tell me what was going on? There came a knock on the door and the High Sage Gretta entered her room with a look of worry on her face that made Linda worried as well.

Gretta asked her how much she remembered about the night of the attempted mind-link with her daughter Daphne. And why would she try such a fool hearted move without waiting for their help. Will someone explain to me what is going on? And why no one will tell me what happened and why her daughter was not with them. Gretta was the first to explain the events of that night and how they had to fight to recover her from the hold of the Dark Lord had on her. After we were able to remove you from the mind-link you crumbled to the floor and we had Tree Mender carry you to your bed. That was over a week ago and we feared we had lost you. What do you mean it has been a week? What happened that you are not telling me about? We heard the screams in the middle of the night and felt the pull of the Dark One's evil when we entered her rooms, we found you in a mind-link with Daphne. We tried to strengthen the link so we could help recover both of you, but the Dark One threw you at us and broke the link before we had a chance to free Daphne.

We tried to reestablish the link to recover the child, but his power was too strong for us. And we were forced to leave her mind without rescuing her.

We were afraid that if we tried to force the Dark One out of her mind, she might lose the battle in her mind and she would lose her sanity. So, what are you saying that my daughter is trapped in her mind? With nothing we can do to free her mind and body. Yes, Night Sage that is what we are saying, but we are trying everything, and we have hope that we will find something soon. In the meantime, my daughter is trapped with him in her mind doing unknown damage to her. What if he can affect her mind and she wind up a puppet of the Dark Lord? What will we do if that happens? She is my child. Daphne had to put up wall upon wall in her mind to shield herself from the on slot of evil that was trying to penetrate her mind. She knew that if she gave up, she would lose her mind, or worse become a puppet of the darkness that was trying to break down her defenses. Daphne prayed to The Forest God to come to her aid and hoped the Sage where doing the same, it looked bleak. But her mother was Linda the Night Sage and she could feel her presence close by. The only thing Linda the Sage could think of was to go to the Forest God and beg for her daughter's life.

She had not been to the crater in close to a thousand years, but she still knew the way and this time she could use her powers. And she planned to shift into a large hawk and covers much more ground than by foot.

Before she could go to her God, she had to make sure the Sage where going to do all they could to protect her daughters poor mind. With a prayer to her God she tried to shift into a hawk and fly as fast to the crater as she could, but someone grabbed her and stopped her. Linda the Night Sage wanted to go alone so that she did not endanger anyone else, but Gretta the High Sage insisted that she bring at least Tree Mender, for he also cared for Daphne's safety and her mind. So, with a quick prayer for her child and their safety on the long trip, they shifted and flew in the direction of the Crater of the Forest God.

Linda and Tree Mender had never been linked before so Linda did a mind-link with him so they could communicate with each other in their hawk form. Being in the form of the hawk made the trip faster, but they still had to shift back to their human form to hunt and make a fire to cook the food from the nights hunt. They took turns to guard each other against the night so no one came upon them in their sleep and decide to rob or kill them. Yes, it had been a thousand years since the Clan Wars but with the Dark One gaining power they did not want to take a chance. They flew as far as they dare by day and at dusk they hunted for food after word they went right away to sleep, with one staying awake to guard over the other. Even traveling as, a hawk they ran into trouble from other birds that attacked them when they entered their air space.

The trip for Linda was going to slow and she was biting at the bit for she dreaded the thought of her daughter in the grips of the Dark One. Tree Mender was her saving grace for he kept her sane along the trip, the High Sage was right about not traveling alone but she would never admit it. Tree Mender was truly a good friend to her, and her daughter and she appreciated him and his company, she always did things alone for after

losing Beaver Tail she could not bring herself to trust anyone with her safety but herself. Being a Sage and being on the council is her life and she loved it but getting out and traveling the same roads from her past brought back fond memories.

She could not afford to get soft she had to rescue their daughter, but she did miss him so. Maybe when this is all over, she could find the time to mourn her only love, the father of her only daughter. No one questioned them about their relationship for they came home victorious and saved them from the dark Lord. Most believed that The Forest God graced her with a child in appreciation for her willingness to aid her God. Either way she was grateful for the time she had with him and now their daughter was in danger from the Darkness that affected their planet over a thousand years ago.

Their God was the strongest of the God's that their people prayed to, but would one God be able to defeat the Dark One after all these years.

Linda slept restless each night of their journey because of the Darkness that took her only child was growing, but this time the Dark One was trying to take over the minds of the faithful and turn them into mindless puppets. It was clear to her what he was up to for she saw his plans when she linked with Daphne, she was able to see enough from the Dark Lords plans and felt his desperation and the feeling that this time everything was different. For he was fighting to the death, his or ours it did not matter he was not going into that prison again. Each night more people were turned into puppets for the Dark One, it did not matter how much you struggled he would not stop until he had your mind under his control. The Sage where one of the ones not affected by his trap that he set each night for they had been praying around the clock since Linda and Tree Mender had left. Many of the simple farmers, crafters, forgers, and many of the trades were affected first and many did not know anything was different about them. Family members could not tell anything was different about their loved ones, until it was too late and they to where under his power. Each night the Darkness entered more dreams until thousands were his puppets without any one even knowing the difference. Linda the Night Sage could feel the pull of evil trying to overcome her each night her and Tree Mender were exhausted every morning from the long nights battle for their minds. Thankfully, they were safe from his influence when they shifted, for some reason they could got all day without any on slot on their minds. At night they had to shift back into human form to hunt and eat and then fall exhausted asleep only to fight each night for their minds. They had no contact with any of the outside world and did not know just how much influence the Dark One now had. Soon he would be strong enough to break free from his prison that he was trapped in all these years.

With all his followers and puppets at his control he would be able to take over about everyone without a fight. Linda just hoped that her people were safe and able to fight against his nightly on slot of their minds and to find a way to slow down the Dark Lords effect on the people of their once peaceful plain and her poor daughter. Soon Linda would be too tired from the struggling in the day to achieve their goal and the nights fighting for their minds and freedom. She just wished there were a way to get to their God that was faster, then it come to her that on her last trip. The Forest God gave her a way to reach him once they got close enough. Linda forgot to pack it, but to her surprise she found it in her pack, thank the God of the Forest for reminding someone to pack it for her. The way it worked if they got to a certain point, they would be transported directly to him without the need to go thru the trials. Linda just hoped that both would be able to use the present that was given to her. It looked like a twisted piece of wood with about one hundred holes in it, when it was turned upside it sounded like rainfall on a roof. When played a certain way it would transport her to her God where they would be safe from the Dark Lords influence. It was hard to tell if they were on the right path sometimes for it had been over a thousand years and trees and shrubs grow to change the land. Also, with hardly any sleep for days on end their minds were cloudy and fuzzy, making it twice as hard to stay on the right pass. Being able to fly made things harder some days for on a cloudy rainy day it became impossible to see yet alone fly. No one likes to be cold and damp for any period and shifting was no protection from the weather. To make things worse on rainy days it was imposable to start a fire to warm up, yet alone find food. With over a thousand years the land had recovered very nicely, and food was plentiful, most people had forgotten about The Clan Wars.

The four Clans had put away their past grievances and got alone better over the years that past. We started to wonder if we were going the correct direction for the map brought was made just after I returned from the last trip to talk to our God. Everyone knows that the suns rise towards the solar sails and sets in the lunar plains, so they can get the correct bearings on sunny days. But it had been harsh weather for over a week now and we have been making little progress up to this point. Our spirits are low, we are cold, tired, and just wish the suns would rise for just a solar cycle so we could dry out and get enough food to quiet our bellies. As if the Forest God graced us with a gift, the rain slowed and then came to a complete stop and the suns shined brightly. The red sky was so beautiful with the way it swirled and changed hue, our bellies were still empty, but we planned to take care of that right away. Tree Mender went out to hunt us up some food, and I pray to our God he brings back some purple pears and green hare for we needed the meat. I attended the camp, set out our cloths to dry and started a fire to cook any meat Tree Mender brought back, and thanked the woods for its protection. With the camp set up I decided to look for herbs that I saw growing wild to season the meat. We ran out over a cycle ago and I for one will not eat any more tasteless food. While looking for herbs to season our dinner I collected some tallow wood and thanked the trees for their gift. As I was walking back to our camp, I came across a Scarlet horned Netter with its paw stuck in a trap, these creatures are some of the oldest and the rarest still rooming the plains. These once great creatures were more plentiful than any other in our lands, until people found out their fur possessed magical qualities. After that the Scarlet Netter was killed not for their meat, but just for their fur, people left the meat to rot on the plains as they cashed in on the Netter's magical fur the they became increasingly rare.

The Magical property on the Netter fur offered them some protection while it hunted, but once removed from the animal it is magic would slowly drain away. Thus, the need for more fur to replace the drained fur and the massive slaughter of the species that once was so many that they dwindled down to a few that were left. The Sage stepped in to keep the Scarlet Horned Netter from being forever removed from the forests and the plains making the first protected species act and made it a serious crime to kill or even wear its fur. This only caused the poachers to become part an underground network that killed and striped the fur from every Netter. Which also made the price for their fur to go higher than ever, for it was now a crime to kill a Netter and they had to take more steps to hide the fur until they sold it on their illegal markets. The penalty for killing a protected species now became a top priority as the council was convened to address the problems that arose trying to protect such a beautiful creature from dying off. The council set up a group of laws that would make any creature that was on their list, a protected animal and the fines would finally stop the Scarlet Horned Netter from being killed off they hoped. But if they could not save the Netter, just maybe they could stop other creatures of their forest and the planes safe for all time. The Sage knew from the start of time that the creatures of the Forest had different magical abilities they used when they hunted, but it never crossed their minds that someone would kill a Forest creature to use its power. After all everything in the forest was created by their God and to kill any of his creatures for anything but food, was against everything they believed in. Outside of their protected forest they had extraordinarily little to make people see their side that the creatures were to be protected for they are gifts from their God. The four Clans each worshiped a different God and their beliefs were vastly different from the other, we in the Forest Clan believed in the protection of the Forest and all its creatures. If an animal was killed it was for food and everyone thanked their God for supplying us the nourishment that we needed to survive.

Linda the Night Sage knew about all the animal of their Forest, but this was not her Forest nor was this a creature that she wished to get close to. Any animal trapped is dangerous and should be left alone, for they are unpredictable when cornered or trapped as this Scarlet Horned Netter was. Linda knew all the animals of their world should be left to their own devices, but this one was trapped in a hunter's trap and will be killed when the poacher came back. Linda's blood boiled for she was on the council that made the protected species act and knew of the plight of the Netter. She had never seen one up close and just heard stories of their beauty, but this one could by the last Netter alive outside of the

Forest where it would be protected. They had a wide area that it hunted for food for it would not eat anything it could get it paws on, it was quite precise about its food and only eat the thorny green hare of the planes.

This Netter was far from the lower planes that were once its home hunting grounds, it must of came all the way out here to get away from the poachers. Linda could shift into a Netter to get its trust and to get close to it and see if it were hurt, but she did not know from this distance if the Netter in front of her was a male or female. If she picked the wrong sex the Netter would kill her on sight for, they are very territorial. Linda could not take the chance if she wanted to save the last Netter, so she decided she would not take the risk and would approach it in her human form. She prayed a quick prayer and walked toward the Netter projecting peaceful thoughts to calm it, so she could get close enough to free it from the trap. The closer she got the Netter would hiss louder towards her, so she prayed harder, she was not going to leave this beautiful creature to die or get killed by whoever left his trap here.

There is no mistake that the Netter was trapped in the trap for it was baited with its favorite food, this was no mistake, not on a mission to save her daughter! She would not let them get away with this, but the trap was simple enough and Linda could remove it without hurting the Netter any more than it already was. She walked forward with her head down in a submissive manner, so she did not get herself killed trying to spare the Scarlet Netter. It worked for the Netter calmed down and realized she was trying to help it, so with one hurdle passed she continued forward until she was inches from its massive paw. The

Scarlet Horned Netter is known for its exceptionally large paws that it uses to capture its pray, but this paw was so large from the trap that snared it left paw. The right paw thou large was not damaged in any way that she could see, so she knew it must be hurting and fearful for its life. Linda slowly reached for the paw in the trap so she could remove the noose and realized the Netter trusted her now so she could remove it without any danger of winding up on its dinner plate. She pulled on the wire that trapped it left paw and released its paw slowly from the trap so as not to alarm it or hurt it any further. Gracefully the Netter pulled out its paw and tried it out to see if it would hold its weight, howling a loud cry I knew it could not be left in this condition to die. Without the use of the paw it could not hunt or kill food for it could not run and would surely die before its paw healed. Linda pulls some of the herbs that she collected on a cloth and wrapped it around the left paw to help it heal faster and bring down the swelling. She had saved its life and now the animal was her responsibility to keep it safe until it could hunt for itself, she just hoped the Netter saw it that way too. Linda coaxed it gently to the spot that they were using as their camp and started a fire with the wood she got prior to finding the Netter stuck in the trap. She called to Tree Mender threw the mind-link that they shared to warn him of their guest and to approach the camp carefully so as not to scare the Netter and becoming its next meal.

Linda was tending to the Netter when she received a message from Tree Mender wanting to know if it was safe to enter the camp. Yes of course it was safe just approach quietly and everything should be no problem, (she hoped.) She spoke in a gentle voice to the Netter that they were to have a friend enter the camp and that there was nothing to get alarmed about. She understood her enough for Linda to be certain Tree Mender would be safe for now, but if you are to be our Guest what am I to call you?

Being a Sage, she had a connection with most animals even if they were not from the protection of their Forest. The Scarlet Netter spoke not to her mind but to her face saying that her name was once called the mighty one by her fellow Netter but she could call her Flaawna. After her first shock wore off what had just happened. Linda could not believe that this intelligent creature was hunted like Orange Flap Cattle, but not for its meat but for its magical fur. Her anger got the best of her for just a minute, and she was surprised by her sudden anger for she had never lost her temper before. Excuse my manners my name is Linda the Night Sage champion of her people, but you can call me I hope your friend someday. So, then Linda it is. When is this person of yours returning?

For I am famished after being in that snare so long, and with my hurt paw I cannot hunt so he better brings enough, or she would eat him for lunch. She laughed so hard she forgot about the pain for just a minute, you should have seen your face. You Forest people need to learn to laugh, and with that they but laughed so much Linda did not see Tree Mender enter the camp. Flaawna did see him and in a low hiss said that had better be your friend the own you call Tree Bender. Linda looked in the direction that Tree Mender came in from and said yes this is a good friend of my family. He has a good heart and is no danger to you

Flaawna, let's hope he is well stocked with food so he does not become lunch With that they broke into a loud laugh, poor Tree Mender did not get the joke and did not want to become any ones lunch especially a Scarlet horned Netter's lunch.

After some laughter at his expense Linda asked, "what did he bring back for lunch?" for our new friend is Hungry? Tree Mender said he was lucky in his hunt and thinks he has enough for all, including a couple of Spiny Green Hare for our friend over there. Without any delay on his part he threw the Hare to Flaawna, and watched with amazement as she finished off the hare with ease. But, with a hunger from her not eating for so long her paw did not slow she down one bit, and he made note of this point in his mind. This was not a fuzzy Greengle Cat from the Forest, it could kill at will if it wished to, he was glad he was not the Spiny Hare. Linda said enough about Spiny. What did you bring for us to eat? And it better not be something slimy or greasy for once, she could not handle any nastier food. Not that she was spoiled, or anything like that she just wanted some plucked chicken of any kind it did not matter if it was Blue Fowl, or Yellow bush Hen. She just wanted to eat some meat that she did not gag on. Flaawna said if you do not want your food that she would eat it, for she may hunt for Spiny Green Hare, she does not always find one. And She had no problem eating anything put before her because she ate everything raw. After everyone was feed, they had to collect more wood for the fire and then bunker down for the night so they could get a start in the morning. Flaawna spoke up at this time and said, "what about me?" I still have this problem of my paw hurting from the trap it was in just a matter of hours ago. She said she could watch over them while they slept so they can get a good night's rest, which it looked as thou, they could use it. Flaawna I am so sorry I forgot that you could not travel yet, do you think that you may be able to travel in a couple of days? Flaawna said that the magical properties that everyone seems to want from my fur, has other abilities of healing. I just need time in the sun to help my magic to work, so as the answer to your question I can travel in one day's time.

Let us pray that it is a sunny day tomorrow for we are on a spiritual quest to save my daughter from the control of the Dark Lord. Linda the Night Sage decided to tell her story of her daughter to Flaawna so she could understand the need for a fast pace to find the Forest God, so he can intervene for her daughter Daphne. Flaawna said with wet eyes that the poachers killed her cubs not too long ago. And that she was still morning their loss, for the poachers also took her mate to be slaughtered for his fur and that she ran so they would not get her as well. Linda was saddened by her loss and the loss of her mate, but if she did not come along why she did Flaawna would have met the same fate. Flaawna shocked them all with the statement that she made next, about Linda saving her from the trap, that she now indebted to her until for the rest of her days living. Flaawna went on to explain that the debt was a blood debt and could not be refused, for she was honor bound and she always paid her debts. Linda and Tree Mender were touched by this announcement, but Tree Mender warned Linda not to refuse for she will not regret it if she did, with her life. Linda got down on her knees and thanked Flaawna, and accepted her generous offer, saying it was her honor and privilege to have a friend like her. Linda stroked the Netter's fur and Flaawna let loose a purr of pleasure, for the Sage hit just the right spot and she was in heaven. Tree Mender was surprised by this exceptionally large creature turning to putty with Linda stroking it is back; he could not believe his eyes. How could anyone kill such a majestic creature that little was known of before today? With no one to find out more of the Scarlet Horned Netter, why it was only that today someone was able to befriend the last of its kind.

CHAPTER V

So how is poor Daphne today? Has there been any change in her condition? Gretta was so worried that what had happened to Daphne was also happening to all the people of the Four Clans. They had not heard anything back from Linda or Tree Mender and were starting to worry for Daphne's mind. For either she would be able to fight off the Dark One's attack on her mind, or she could be lost in the Dark void of what was to be left of her mind. Each day that past brought her closer to the Dark Lord for her mind could only take so much, before she had to give in.

The Sage prayed over her each day and continued the round the clock vigil over her, but they were also dealing with the many others that the Dark One had overcome. The Four Clans reported that so many people had fallen into a coma state and no matter what they did they could not wake even one person. People from all over their lands were becoming afraid of falling to sleep, for they might not wake in the morning. The current tally was two hundred minds that had been taken over and with them no closer to stopping the Dark Ones power over their people's minds. No one knew just how long they had before the Dark Army would rise and do the bidding of the Dark Lord as his puppets. Would a brother kill his own sister for she had become part of the Dark Army?

How would a father be able to fight the effects of the mind control before he slaughtered his own family? No matter how bad things looked there was still hope that the God's would step in and destroy the Dark Lord. So, he could never try to break out of his prison and kill again.

What the people of the Four Clans did not understand was that you could not have good without evil, for there had to be a balance in power or everything would cease to exist.

Daphne was fighting the battle of her young life to keep the Dark Lord from taking over her mind and turning her into a puppet for his puppet army. She was so tired of fighting so hard each day to keep up the many walls that she had built in her mind.

If things did not change soon, she did not know how much more she could hold on. For with each wall she added he destroyed ten more, she had no idea how long she had been fighting the battle for her sanity and her freedom from his dark plans. Daphne may be trapped in her mind, but she was not going to just give up for she was the daughter of the Night Sage. Her mother would never stop until she saved her, so Daphne had a duty to her mother and the Sage to fight the Darkness that wanted to take control of her mind. Up to this point Daphne had been trying to run from her would be captor, he would not expect her to go on the offensive. She was a fighter not someone to run away from her problems but what could she do to stop the Dark Ones trap. With no one being able to bring her out the maze that she built in her mind, she could help in some way to overcome the trap in her mind. Surely, she was not the only one fighting to overcome the effects of the Dark One's plans, could she find a way of stopping his plans from inside her mind? She had to fight back some way, or she would lose the battle that was raging for control for her mind, but what she had no idea. But she would test the walls of the prison in her mind to find if there were cracks or holes that she could escape threw or set a trap of her own. With her newfound strength and a plan, she set forth to overcome her captor and help others to fight for control of their minds and bodies. Fighting from the inside was better than not fighting at all so she set forth to find the limits of her mind, and to find ways to put a couple of well-known thorns in his behind. The more she fought him the less he would want to capture her mind for there were others out there that he could turn into puppets with less trouble. Whatever her fate was she was sure of one thing eventually good always conquered over evil, and she planned to do her part.

The Sage would never stand for their people becoming puppets and she was sure they were doing everything they could think of. She also knew that her mother Linda the Night Sage would be on her way to request council with the Forest God and request for him to step in and stop the Dark ones plans for good. Speaking of her mother there was some way for Daphne to communicate with her mother, threw the Mind-Link that was performed on her not to long ago. But how? Maybe if she thought hard enough upon her mother's face, she could send her a message?

What could it hurt to try? Nothing was the answer that Daphne produced, so she focused all her thoughts on her mother until the link was restored. After much time and energy Daphne felt her mother near and spoke to her in her mind, but would she be able to talk back to her over the distance. If Daphne let down too many walls in her mind, so her mother could get thru to her she could leave herself open to attack. It was a risk she had to take, for her mother may know of a way to release her from her prison that Daphne made to keep out the Dark one. She sent out a thought to her mother without knowing if it would work, but when this was all over, she would ask her mother more about how the Mind-Link worked. Now she had to make the Dark One so uncomfortable in her mind she could take advantage of him to cause as much damage as possible. As she waited to see if her mother got her message threw the link, she would do everything she could think of to fight back, until she was released from her mind. She had no way of knowing how long she was trapped or no way of reaching out to the Sage that must be very worried. If she could somehow send them a message to let them know that she has not given up. But who could she send a message to for if she were correct Tree Mender would be with her mother and she did not know many Sage in Training yet?

Wait maybe if she sent a message to someone with more powers, she would have a better chance for success. What other Sage had enough powers to receive her message? Yes! That was it; she could send a message to the mind of the High Sage Gretta for with her mother gone she was the next highest Sage. With all her inner strength she reached out to Gretta in her mind hoping she would be able to hear her plea.

Gretta was in her office looking thru all the books she had gathered, to try to help get Daphne back, when suddenly she felt a bump in her mind. But it did not make any sense to her, so she ignored it and went back to the book she was reading. Then it was there again, much harder, and clearer than the last, and she stopped what she was doing. What is it?

And why are you trying to get into my mind? She found herself saying aloud without meaning to. And to her shock, she knew this to be Daphne but how? Gretta can you hear me? It is Daphne, please hear me, came to her over and over in her mind. Yes, child I can hear you, but how are you doing this? For you are down the hall in your room trapped with the Dark One in your mind, are you not? Yes, came the remark from Daphne in the mind of Gretta's. How is it that you can communicate with my mind? I cannot explain it right now, but I wanted to express that I am ok, and I plan to fight the Dark One's powers over my mind until I am successful. Pray for me, was the last thing Gretta heard and knew Daphne had left her mind. We are child more than you can know, back in her own mind, she was pleased by the luck she had up to this point, but she longed for a word from her mother. With every Wall that Daphne put up in her mind she started to put alarms or traps for her captor the Dark One. She had to be careful about what she was doing so she did not fall in any traps herself for that is what got her here in the first place.

Daphne was excited about her newfound powers that helped her communicate even if it is only a couple of feet, if she practiced some more, she should increase the range. Linda and Tree mender were able to continue their journey with Flaawna following close behind guarding their rear from attack. With the new member to their quest they shifted into something better suited for their new friend, they choose the Red Speckled War Horse for its power and speed. They still run wild in the high planes on the far side of Wardar their home planet grazing on the purple grasses from the start of our time. Flaawna was not comfortable with them shifting into her species so they decided to use the War Horses. They would need because of their speed, but also to push Flaawna into using her damaged paw more each day. Linda was pleased by the new arrangement they had with Flaawna for it turns out that she is a much better a hunter then Tree Mender, so she took over the job of feeding their motley little group. As far as she could remember they should be getting closer to the Crater of Fire where their God should be. The magical devise that her God had given her had a small radius that it would work, and in a couple of days they should be in range for Linda to use it. All she could think about was her daughter and if she were safe or a mindless puppet of the Dark Lord, God she prayed that she was safe and ok. When she able to get any sleep without the Dark thoughts flooding her mind and trying to make her into his slave. Also Came thoughts of her daughter pleading with her to answer her over and over, it was as thou she stumbled upon a way to communicate with just her mind. This made her wonder if it were possible to communicate with someone's mind without a link, she would have to try this out for herself when all this was over. Why can't things go back to way it was before the Dark Lord started to break out of his confines and start another War.? Linda was getting too old for this kind of traveling and things were starting to bother her more with each day, but she had to brush them off so she could complete her mission.

After all this she could request time off from the Counsel, for she was going to need a break after all this. She knew one thing, traveling was for the young, man was she ever hurting in places she never hurt before. If not for the fact she thought that they were close to reaching their goal, she would suggest a day off to recover from the fast pace they were on. By her judging of their position they could not be more than two or three solar rotations of their Three Suns until they reached their goal. Back in the Forest more and more accounts came in each day of the Dark One's work, people were going to sleep at night and never waking, as thou they were waiting for orders People were afraid to go to sleep for they did not want to wind up as mindless puppets in the Dark Army that was growing with each night. The council was overrun with people wanting safety from the Dark Ones influences and if they were doing anything to keep them safe. The council held an emergency meeting to find some way to keep their people safe, but after hours of deliberation they were no closer than when they started. They all came to the same conclusion, that they could only pray for Linda and Tree Mender would be successful in alerting the God of the Forest to their cause. Daphne was on everyone's mind and the fight of her young life; would she be the same person as before the Dark Lord tried to enter her mind. The only person that knew of Daphne's plight was Gretta the High Sage for Daphne herself found a new way of communicating with her threw her mind. Not a Mind-Link but different and the only one that knew how to perform it was trapped in her mind, fighting off the Dark One power in her mind. Gretta was a nervous wreck for all she could do is pray and waits for news from Daphne or her mother, she wished something would happen sooner than later. It was easy to fight someone you could see, but going into your mind while some one slept, how do you defend against that? Little did anyone know Daphne was doing just that, fighting a battle for her mind and she life if she was not careful.

Instead of waiting for someone to save her, she went on the offense and was doing her small part to defend against the Dark Lord and his powers. If she could find a way to reach into the mind of the Dark One, she could do to him what he is doing too many others in their lands. But how could she get into his mind without him finding out and stopping her before she could do some damage to the one that keeps affecting their lives in the worse ways. She had to try some way to stop him or keep him from hurt more people and turning them into his puppets. But what could she do to stop him while she is trapped herself? That was the answer, yes it had to work it was the only way for her to stop him, even if it cost her life. Linda the Night Sage was traveling with Tree Mender and Flaawna there newest addition to their group, she was not certain where they were for so much has changed over the thousand years since she was here last. Flaawna was a little ahead of them acting as scout and their early warning system, she insisted that she was a better scout then them and they had to agree. Then all the sudden Linda heard a strange noise coming from her backpack and called everyone over to check it out. None of them had the faintest idea what it could be, so they decided to open the pack and find out what it could be. With as much care as she could she stuck in her hand and pulled out the devise that when played right it would teleport the user to the home of their God. It was buzzing and quivering like it had something it wanted them to see, in her hands it came alive and played a short tune. That at the time Linda was in a clearing and them the next thing she saw was their God of the Forest standing in front of her with the biggest smile on his face. She could not believe her luck, for after all this time it took to get here, she finally was able to talk to the only one that could help her and her people. She bent down before her God in reverence and respect for his power that one could see was coming from him that there was no doubt that the was a God standing before her. She had not seen him in close to a thousand cycles and yet it seemed as thou it was just yesterday.

In a big booming voice came a laughter that Linda was not expecting, for she did not think he would be happy to see her. How is the Sage that is called Linda? Is the world in trouble again? I hope that troublemaker that I put away so many cycles ago is not up to his old tricks again. With a smile on her face she replied that yes, he is and that is the why she came to see him, after all these years. The Dark One is trying to raise an army by attacking people's minds and making them into puppets waiting to do his will, when he calls for them. So, what is his plan? What does he plan to do with these puppets when he is ready to call forth his army of mindless puppets? I am not sure what his plan is my Lord, but I do know that he has enough puppets or people under control he has affected their minds and plans to cause quite a lot of trouble. The main reason that I came looking for you is because he has tried to take control of my daughter Daphne. She is fighting off his powers but, I do not know how much longer she can hold out from becoming his next puppet to add to his collection. Fear not my child I the God of the Forest will protect my people and the others under his control, but first I need an assistant who can give me all the details. You helped me once are you up for the challenge this time? For you are much older and I hope wiser with the years that have passed Sage. Yes, my Lord I am up to the task, but I should tell you that I did not come alone. I brought two friends with me that could be of use to you. One of which is a Scarlet Horned Netter who likes to be called Flaawna, and the other is a close friend of my daughter. Both I trust with my life as well as the life of my daughter Daphne. Tree Mender is her bodyguard for all intensive purpose, for Daphne. She also has the gift of seeing visions of the Dark One, and his doings as I once did.

That could come in handy if she were not trapped in her mind; we must that care of that at once.

I can transport you, but your friends may have to wait a little longer for I have a mission for them, if they are up to the task. Call for them, for I wish to speak to them before we travel to my Forest, for I have a plan that if it works may find the Dark One sleeping. Linda the Night Sage went to retrieve her friends so that she could guide them into the crater that housed a living God. When got to the outer region of the Crater and to the area that she had left them to find out that no one was there. She called out to them and no reply came to her and after looking around she found big tuffs of fur and human blood. If something happened to them, she would not forgive herself. Where they followed? Or did someone just decide to make a fast fortune by selling them. Chances are that they were stumbled upon by a group of poachers, who grabbed Flaawna for her fur and Tree Mender was just a bonus. She tried to reach Tree Mender thru her Mind Link and there was no reply, what could have happened to them? She returned to the crater that held her God in tears and sobbing something that was sobbing than words. The God of the Forest could not understand her and told her to get a grip on herself so he could find out what was wrong with the Sage women. Where are your friends? Did you not go out to get them, so where are they? Linda regained her control and felt ashamed of herself for losing her control in front of her God of all Beings. She apologized for her loss of her control and went on to tell of what she saw when she returned to the clearing where she left her friends. She would never have thought anyone would follow them, but chances are they were followed. But followed by whom? And who would have been able to take on a full grown Scarlet Horned Netter and Tree Mender without some dead being left behind?

That is when the Forest God spoke and said, "it could have been none other than the Dark Lords work" But how could they not notice someone following them? For Flaawna would have heard someone or smelled someone in the area, right?

So how could the Dark Lords followers find them unless... No, she could never believe that in a Million Cycles. Could she have been set up? No, she would never believe one of her own could be a spy or worse working for the Dark lord, and she never noticed it after all this time.

How could one of the Dark Ones followers slip into her company and her not realize it? Was Tree Mender a spy? or was it their new friend Flaawna the Scarlet Netter? At this time, her God stepped into her thoughts and tried to offer a unique perspective to what may have happened and what to do now. Do we go after your friends, or do we save your daughter who could become a pawn for the Dark One in any time? Which one is in more danger? And who do you try to save first? I am a God, I can transport you to either place, but I cannot save all your people at once. You must choose who to save first and doing so you may be risking the lives of the ones you do not pick. So, miss Linda of the Sage where are we going? And you better pick well, for your friends or your Daughter may perish if you chose wrong. So where are we

heading? Linda the Night Sage was for the first time in her life confused as to what she should do for she had no desire for anyone dying because of her poor choose. Why was this happening to her? How could she choose over her daughter or her friends? She could not choose, there had to be another way but what was it and how could she be in two places at once. Wait! That was the answer.

Back in the mind of Daphne, the daughter of a Sage was now in a pinch, for if she could not think of something soon she may very well loose her battle for her mind and become a puppet of the Dark One.

Daphne was not going to give in to some fly by night petty God that must pray on the minds of the weak to be able to gain control of people's minds. She was stronger willed and is the daughter of Linda the Night Sage, who with our God of the Forest was able to defeat the Dark God.

She was always getting into trouble, and not taken seriously up to a short while ago, so why not use some of her mischief to overcome the trap in her mind. She thought she could do more work to stop the Dark One in the safety of her mind, but now she realizes she could do more damage to him outside the protection of the walls in her mind.

Somehow, she had to break out of her mind and hurt the Dark One at the same time. How could she do as much damage to the Dark Lords plans? And return to the world she loves without losing her mind in the process. She could reach out to the High Sage Gretta and see if she found some way for her to leave her mind yet? She still was able to reach out to her and receive information about the outside world, and the progress they should have on removing her from her mind. She reached out with her mind and sought out the mind of Gretta the High Sage, she found it easier with each time she tried. Gretta was glad to hear Daphne's voice in her head, for she knew she was safe and still fighting for what is rightful hers her mind. Gretta conveyed to the child she knew her whole life that there was no word from Tree Mender or her mother, but she expected to hear something soon. Gretta did have an idea of how Daphne could regain her mind, but it would be risky, and it could not work at all. Or worse it could leave her mind open to attack from the Dark one and his evil plans to make her into his puppet.

Gretta would never forgive herself if something went wrong, and then had to tell Linda her mother what happened and that it was her idea.

Daphne was able to communicate through what she called a bump or a tap of the mind of the person she wished to talk to. She still had to figure out just how she did it, but for now all she knew was it worked. She did learn that for it to work the person that she wished to talk to had to be close enough for her mind to reach out and bump. So far Gretta was the only one that she was able to communicate with, but she did not try hard to extend her reach. But now she could feel something was very wrong and she needed more than ever to get herself back so she could find out what was wrong in the outside world. Lord please let nothing be wrong with my mother for she could not live with something happening to her or Tree Mender. She practiced more each day and night to send her mind bump farther and more powerful so she could find out what was wrong. It came to her at last, how to break out of her mind and the trap that held her fighting him off up to this moment. She had to be careful about her plan. If it did not work it could cost her mind and make her a puppet of the Dark one. She had been going about this the whole time; instead of retreating into her mind she needed to fight for her freedom. So, she made it her mission to create as many problems for the Dark One and attack his mind for he was not yet at full strength or he would not still be in his prison. If she was correct and the Dark Lord was still weak in this plain, then she could break out but first she must make a diversion. This way his mind would be fixed somewhere else and he would not notice her being gone until it was too late, but what would be a big enough distraction. A frontal assault would not work, for it would only make him try harder to keep her under his control. She had to be sly and find a way for her to escape without losing her mind in the process, but what could it be? If only there was some way to trick him in believing she was still trapped while she slipped out of his grasp.

There is more than one way to skin a Spiny Green Hare, and she was going to find out what it was for her life depended on it, as well as all the others the Dark One turned into puppets. Could she somehow figure out a way to escape and recover not just her mind but others as well?

She needed a way to pull it off and recover as many captives as well, she could trick him into thinking that Daphne escaped and then when he let down his guard she would escape for real. That was it, it could be no simpler then convincing the Dark Lord that his puppets had escaped and then she would make her move. She had been working on her mind bump and she had gotten good at it, now it was time to kick it up a notch and see what she was made of. If she concentrated with her whole mind including the walls of protection, she held up this whole time she should be able to do it. She focused all her thoughts towards the Dark Lord and planting a vision in his mind of people fleeing in every direction it may work. But first she needed to bump Gretta's mind and ask her for the extra power she would need to pull this off. Once she felt her power flow toward her, she would start her plan, it may take more than Gretta alone. She would need all their strength to pull it off, she prayed to her God for strength and for his guidance to help this work. She thought of the Dark One and reached out to his mind so she could implant a thought of his puppets fleeing in every direction and his power over them waning and drain his power long enough to pull off her plan. It was like she just banged her head against a rock, she would need all their strength to plant her suggestion in his mind. It was working, but he was much more powerful than she expected, and called out to the Forest itself to come to her aid and fight her fight. Daphne could feel something starting to give from the direction of the Dark Lords prison and hoped that it would not take too much longer for she could feel her strength failing her. She had never held on to so much power in her whole life, this had to work.

Wait she could feel a crack in his mind, a bend in his armor so to speak and that was all she needed, she widened that crack and made it large enough for her mind suggestion to take hold in his mind. The next thing that happened she had been waiting for a long time, she sat up and found herself in her rooms surrounded by Sage worried and glad she was finally free of the Dark Ones trap. And to their surprise many of the

Forest clan that was trapped puppets of the Dark Lord was waking up also. A little at a time as thou it was just a bad dream, her plan worked but to what price? For the Dark One would be after her more than ever now. The first thing Daphne thought of was her mother ok, and if anyone had heard from Tree Mender or her mother Linda the Night Sage. The answer that she received was not what she would have expected in a thousand cycles that they heard nothing back from her mother. And then she was told that a group of mercenaries had kidnapped Tree Mender, and a Scarlet Horned Netter whatever that was? She must try to reach

Tree Mender with her mind bump if possible, for she had not sent a mind bump far before. She asked the Sage to lend her their power one more time to see if she could reach her friend Tree Mender if he was not dead by now. She sent out her bind bump towards her friend to see if she could reach him and find out if he is ok? But just when she thought about Tree Mender to send her bump, her mother came to her mind and before she could stop it out went her mind bump to the wrong person. To her surprise, she made contact but was it her mother for she had never had one of her mind bumps go arise. She carefully probed the mind that she reached to find out if the mind she reached was indeed her mother's, and what came back left no doubt who it was. The voice in her head came as a shout that she had to turn down so she could explain. "I do not know how you did this, but I am Linda the Night Sage and I do not take lightly to someone messing around with her mind.

Yes, it was her mother all right, it is my mother it is Daphne your daughter and I am ok; I am free of the Dark powers that imprisoned me.

Sorry for not warning you that I was entering your mind but to be truthful I do not know how to do it anyway. I was reaching out to Tree mender and got you by mistake, I will explain how I am able to reach your mind without a mind link I call it a mind bump. I can do it surprisingly good at short range but longer I need help of others to aid me. How are you? Is Tree Mender with you? We heard that he was taken by mercenaries that work for the Dark Lord and they have some creature with him called a horned something. We were hoping that he was with you and not captured, we do not know where he is being held, and to be honest I am worried mother. Honey don't be worried for I am with the Forest God and we are going to make things back the way they should be, and the dark one will receive a good lashing from me about touching one of the Sage for we are protected by our God directly. Our God is not happy that he must deal with the Dark One again so soon after he put him away last time. Yes, time travels faster for a God then it does for us, a thousand cycles are a blink of their eye to them. It is good to know where Tree Mender and that horned something's name is Flaawna and you will love her, but you should go now for you will be very tired and want to sleep for days to regain your strength. I love you and I will talk to you soon; we will take care of those mercenaries on our way back to the forest. Rest now! And with that the bump was gone and her mother was right she could sleep for days, she was so tired... Yawn. I am so sleepy. With that Daphne was taken to her rooms and placed on her bed while a guard watched over her.

Daphne was asleep for barely a couple minutes of the cycle when she was attacked by the Dark One, but this time it was personal for she had caused him many puppets. He was going to get them back with or without her, either way he was going to make her pay for what she did. He needed every puppet he could capture in their dreams and enslave them as his army of mindless soldiers, and he was starting with Daphne as his prize puppet. He was watching the thoughts in her mind and overheard a conversation that Daphne had with her mother and decided it was time to go on the offensive. If they thought he was going to roll over and beg for mercy than they we are very mistaken, for with the power from his army of puppets he could equal any god. If he could get rid of a few thrones in his side, then he would be ready to start his "War of the Gods" as it would be called many cycles later. All good Generals needed good officers under their command, and he planned to make his first Captain from one of his enemies. If he could get Daphne under his control it might make up for the puppets she released. With her in a weakened state he should have no problem claiming her for his puppet army; she will do nicely in his collection. He had to be careful about his plan were to fail, he would never get this chance again, if he went to fast in her mind she would wake. The Dark Lord was not going to make any mistakes for this specimen was valuable enough for him to approach her again after so little time had passed since his last try. Daphne was the daughter of the Night Sage who he despised for she helped to secured him in this prison. He wanted out of it bad enough to start a War amongst the God's, that he could not loose for he was not going to be trapped for another thousand cycles. This is his ticket out and he planned to use it, to his full extent but he needed a little more time to gather his army together, with his key players including Daphne.

He could not wait another night she was to be his tonight he approached her mind slowly for he did not want to set off her alarms or wake her before he had her. He went oh so lightly into her mind, to find that with her being so tired she left her mind wide open to attack. This was going to be so simple; he could taste sweet success she was to be his, and he entered her thoughts so overconfident he missed an alarm that Daphne set. Right before she went to sleep, she placed a mental alarm in her mind to keep from becoming a puppet of the Dark Lord.

She would have wakened upon a sound of her trap being sprung, but the Dark Lord was lucky tonight for she was so tired she did not wake and slept on. He had to be more careful if he planned to make her his captain of his puppet army, no more mistakes. Gingerly he went ahead on into her mind until he was within reach of the prize when he saw another trap that Daphne left for him. The Dark Lord was getting terribly upset and without looking for any more traps he charged into her mind with his power she was his to take, until he felt someone attacking him, trying to stop him from entering any further in her mind. What kind of trap was this and who set it for it was not Daphne that set it, if he did not stop this attack from some unknown source, she would wake any minute? Daphne did not know that Gretta the High Sage had placed that trap in her mind that was saving her from the Dark powers that where turning people into puppets. This trap was more sophisticated than any other in her mind that night and from the looks of it he would not be able to decipher and remove it before she woke. He has no choice but to come back another night, No! No Way was he going to be outsmarted by a group of sage, so he progressed forward deeper into her mind removing one trap after another. He was about to the point in her mind where there was no stopping him, when the impossible happened

Just before the inner cortex of her mind a strong voice addressed him and told him "if he did not leave her mind he would be forced to leave." Before he had a chance to reply he was no longer in her mind, for he was thrown out with such a force he never saw it coming. What was in her mind that could throw around a God and remove him from her mind?

What he had no idea was that what had thrown his from the mind of his victim was no magic that he could understand, for it was the pure Love a Father had for his daughter. Even thou Beaver Tail had never met his daughter he pledged to watch over her, and no matter what would come along he would keep her safe. The Dark One was fuming mad, for what or who had the difficulty to man handle him like he was but a toy in a child's hand.

CHAPTER VI

Captain of his dark forces, the love a father has for his child expands all boundaries. For even thou one's body ceases to be and is buried, there essence or what makes them live goes on, some calls this a soul or one's spirit. What you call it in one place does not transcend or go beyond someone's idea of what it means to them, in their time or their plane.

The idea of something not passing on after death has long been part or every generation from the beginning of our known time. It was nothing for Linda to believe, for Beaver Tail always watched over her so why not their daughter Daphne. Beaver Tail died before seeing the birth of his daughter, but on another plane part of him was there her whole life protecting her when he felt it was necessary. Linda felt it in her bones that there was something going on in the Forest that they all loved. She did not know what or who it was happening to but was relieved when she felt the presence of something very dark get thrown from their forest home. She still too far away to know what happened but when she returns, she was going to find out. And may the Dark Lord protect the force she felt for there would be no stopping her if one of her people was harmed in her Forest. She was the Night Sage and it was part of her job to protect it and was so glad that a force of goodness was over her family that night. What Daphne and her mother did not know that Beaver Tail was asked by the very God of their Forest to protect everyone when he was not able. Beaver Tail was no God, but he was no longer human either, so whatever he was did not matter if he could watch over his family. When he died a certain God offered him a deal that he could not refuse, and with no more human limitations he was ideal for the job.

Some I guess would call him a ghost or spirit, but in truth he was no more either of those things for he was given his abilities by a God.

What he was he himself did not know, in the beginning he wanted to know what and how, now he just calls himself blessed. So now you know someone's secret on how he can protect a large Forest without having to be there every cycle of the day. If something happened, he was called upon to handle the grandiose things, but the smaller things he leaves to his right-hand man. For now, he is not worshiped and no he never will be, not even as a lesser God for no one knows he exists, and he is happy that way. He does not go around playing God, besides how could he get any peace with all. That noise that people make crying out for a God, prayers or whatever you call them it is not for him. The God of the Forest is up to his arms full of the mess that was dropped into his lap. How to gather a small attack force to save Tree Mender and Flaawna from their captors? Yes, he is a God, but he must follow a guideline of how and when he can interfere. For yes even a God must follow the rules, when to step in and cause a big ruckus and when it is more diplomatic. You cannot have your people all the time freaking out, for their God touched something of theirs and they will never wash it ever again. After a while things would start to smell and that would never do. Back to the point at hand how to form a rescue party with no one around for miles. I guess I will have to intervene this one time, but you can never tell anyone that I the Forest God did not follow his own rules. Now how are we going to collect a small army to take on the Dark Ones followers and free your friends? How would be the best way? Let me see I could cause a great breeze to blow them away; not when your friends would blow away too.

That will never do for it would cause too much attention; we need something that people will not think make your kind think a God stepped in. This is the reason that I stay in a creator in the farthest point of our land, all the daily decisions can drive a God eccentric.

Let me try something different, Linda the Sage do you have any idea on how to free them without it looking like I played favorites among my own people?

This way if something goes wrong with the plan I will not be blamed, you are old enough to remember the last time that my people blamed me for something going wrong. Linda did not speak the first idea that she thought of, for it was to wait for someone to just walk along that could do our bidding. No that would never do for many a different reason, we do not have the time to just wait around, less the time it would take a God to stop laughing. We could use part of it and ask him if he could see anyone nearby and ask them to hurry to our aid. That may have some merit if, someone is just hanging around to rescue a group of people that got captured by the Dark Lord's men. After thinking for a while about her answer she produced a plan that may just work if he (our God) could speed up time and transport just me threw time. I can shift into the fastest animal that I can think of, so our Lord can make a flurry of wind taking me to the edge of our Forest for help. No that would never work, why can you not give me a devise that would transport me threw time and back with an army. Going thru Time itself is very tricky yet alone how much time it would take to fashion a such device. And making the devise large enough to transport a small army back through, would take forever. If I was not a God and time does not affect me like it does you human, your plan may just work.

I will let you figure out how you got it and how you knew how to work it? That is not up to me, for as the God of the Forest I am not able to speak in half truths. What kind of a God would that make me? Give me some time to fashion you a devise to bend time and bring you back on command. It will seem as though not much time has passed, how much? I do not know, for when you are working with time it can be tricky. You will either have your item, or you will have to produce a different plan we will soon see.

When I come back with the item that will take you thru time, no one, and I mean no one outside the High Sage Gretta and you can ever know of it. Once a God makes something it cannot be undone and that is why the secrecy is so necessary no one can ever find out about it, so it cannot be stolen and misused. If you cannot keep it secret and promise that no other than yourself and the High sage can ever now it exists? There is no point in going on any further, do you swear it you will follow my guidelines? The people that you go to get cannot ever know what you used, so you better hide it well Linda the Sage. No person may ever know it exists for it could unravel time itself if used by the wrong people, do I had to show you what I mean, or do you get the hint? I took an oath when I became a Sage to serve you and do your will, I will not go back on that oath while I live. Ok now that the ground rules are in place you will not see me for a period, remember I as a God am not subjected to the laws of time, so worry not I will be back in no time. Linda the Night Sage was subject to time and it seemed like hours before her God returned with a small object. What is that? Is that going to be able to transport a whole army? I know that you are a God and all, but I cannot help but wonder if it will be big enough. Do you doubt my abilities child?

Remember that I am a God and the size of something does not gauge the power of an item, when you believe in me anything is possible as for, I am God. A God is nothing without people that believe in them, for the power of player can move mountains, you still believe in me do you not?

Of course, I do my Lord I apologize for doubting you; please will you show me how to work the item that you worked so hard to make for my use. I made it as simple as possible while making it look as though it has no special power at all.

Since you are to be the only one to work it, I wanted to make it look as plain as possible so it anyone did find it, they would think nothing of it.

The way it works only a Sage can use it for it requires that the user be pure in heart and body and must be a believer of the Forest God to use it. Just think of where you wish to go and you think of where you want to go, and you will appear that spot. Linda the Sage you need to choose your location carefully for you do not want to have to explain how you just happened to show up in the middle of a group of people. It is best if you appear in a spot away from anyone, and then walk back to the spot you wish to be. It may not be what you want to do as far as where walking back awhile so they are not seen, but there are those of the Dark Ones followers that would love to get their hands on this. Under short notice it will work for what you need it to do, just do not get caught using it for the wrong party would love to have a toy like this. Linda the Night Sage took the item in her hand it looked like fine worked silver, when you looked again it looked like a lump of charcoal and she almost dropped it. For she did not realize what had happened the object in her hand had magical properties to protect itself. She carefully put it in her coin purse to keep it safe until she was ready to use it. At that point, the Forest God says, "why are you still here." So, without any prompt, I said goodbye and took out the object from my purse, it was as thou a lump of charcoal had come alive in my hands and transformed into a shiny silver disk. I concentrated on the field outside of our forest and the next thing I knew I was flat on my back in the weeds in a field I knew all too well. I walked around the corner and was at the entrance of our Forest, as I walked, I returned the lump of coal to my bag.

A shout came forth that the Night Sage has returned to us, but she is alone without Tree Mender in tow. She was escorted to the High Sages outer office for there was a standing order, as soon as Linda the Night

Sage entered the Forest grounds, she was to be brought straight to Gretta the High Sage. After hugs and refreshments, the guards were ordered to leave them for Gretta was dying to find out what happened and where is Tree Mender?

I no more than finished telling the High Sage what had happened there was a knock on the door. Gretta was about to shout they were not to be disturbed, when she remembered about Daphne and how she was dying to see her mother after all the time she was gone. Daphne ran in and put her arms around her mother and gave her a big hug, for she was so proud of her for going all the way she did to rescue her beloved daughter.

Mother I am so glad to see you, as you can see, I am no longer the captive of the Dark One, I was able to break his hold on me with my new mind powers. Since you were gone, I was able to communicate with Gretta the High Sage with my mind while I was fighting the pull of the Dark Lord. I will tell you all about it, wait where is Tree Mender? Did he go to his room already? No child he did not make it back for he and a friend that we were traveling with was taken by the Dark one's men and I do not know where they are? No mother this cannot be, how did this happen? You we are with the Forest God; did they no go with you to see the God of our people? No Daphne they were not in his presence only I could enter in to see the Forest God. But fear not for we were just talking about a rescue plan that the Forest God himself produced.

Please do not blame anyone for the Dark Lord has spies everywhere, these are the ones that stole up Tree Mender and Flaawna. Tree Mender will not be harmed right away but Flaawna is a Scarlet Horned Netters an endangered animal, that its fur is very prized in some circles. Yes, they kill the Netters just for the magical powers of the fur, which the power only lasts for a brief time after the Netters are killed. So, you see she one of the last and they would not hesitate to offer the creature off to the highest bidder. So, Daughter we have no time to lose for both of their lives in danger until we rescue them, this is going to be a short visit, I fear. For as soon as I can gather up some people to rescue them we will be leaving the next day, but with permission from the High Sage you may be able to go with, if Gretta says you are healthy enough to go.

Your new ability will come in handy; I believe you may be able to tell us if they are well and what direction they we are taken. We will be up late going over all the details and who all to take, I will want to talk more about your success with your new mind powers and how they will help the cause. So, go off to bed for we will need you to be alert and fresh in the morning to show us how everything works with your power to speak to someone over vast distances. My Mother was always going about Sage business, so I am ok with not seeing much of her from time to time. She always makes ways to be with me but going with her was something I would not have thought possible up to a brief time ago. What should I bring to a rescue of the only friend that I have had for many years; my mother was correct that I go to my rooms early? Daphne woke earlier than she would on her own for the two Suns were vet to rise, so it must be hours before her normal time she got up. Thank the God that her breakfast was brought with plenty of hot java beans to help her wake.

As if on cue her mother was at her door of her rooms just after she finished her last hot java bean, Daphne I hope you took me seriously last night for I need you at your best. Go ahead and go thru any mental preparations you may need to do, feel free to practice any steps that help you to gather your new powers. After some mental prep Daphne was ready to show her mother how she communicated without a Mind-Link. Daphne explained the steps that brought her to be able to talk to someone's mind and hear them from a distance without using her mouth. She shared how in her desperation to stop the Dark One from taking over her mind she was able with practice she was able to communicate over short spaces. She told her Mother that she thought of the person that might have enough power to receive her message from the heart of her mind.

She knew that Gretta the High Sage would be the one with the most power so she would try to reach out to her first; she was desperate at the time. But she learned how to finesse her power without being in danger of losing her mind, in many ways. She got good at communicating with Gretta and went on to branch out to other people in the Sage but was respectful to only use the ones approved by Gretta herself. It was easy with the High Sage for she was more receptive, with being around magical items and the magical sorts it was not new to her. Being the direct mouthpiece of a God to his people, did have something to do with her choice. Her mother asked Daphne if she had any luck with using her mind bump to any distance and how far she was able to project her mind in reaching out and far as she could go. Daphne only had limited ability at this time, but she was sure that with some more practice she could go farther each time. Well that will have to do for now, I want you to go with you can be our secret weapon, from now on I will be your test subject.

When it is proper to do so I will be the scout in the mission to save our friends and you will be able to practice on your distance a little more each day. As soon as we round up some qualified individuals for our rescue mission we will go as soon as we produce a plan to remove our friends from the control of the Dark one's evil army. Yes that is what he has been up to he is amassing an army to help him first break out then he will want revenge on the ones that put him in the dungeon that he so must want out of. We all must be on our guard for the Dark One has soldiers everywhere and it is only going to get worse until we can stick him back in the box he crawled out of. The Forest God knows of the Dark Lords plans at this time and I am sure that he will be victorious over the Darkness that had affected our once beautiful world. We are safe in our forest paradise, but the rest of our world is not so lucky, when we leave our forest home you all will see the damage that has been done by his Dark hand.

And what it has done to cause destruction to our world, and our once beautiful lands. Do not let the destruction and gloom of the planet effect you or you can become open prey for the Dark Lords plot to affect as many of us, as he can before he breaks himself out of his prison. Go to your room daughter and prepare for the up and coming trip, your role in all this could be major in the contact and rescue of your friend Tree Mender. I just pray that Flaawna is ok for she is one of the last of her kind and a good friend to me and Tree Mender as well; you will like her let us pray that she is ok.

We pick up with Linda the Night Sage in the office of Gretta the High Sage: you are a good friend daughter but I fear that something may go wrong with your trip if we do not hand pick your people for this trip. Which means we are going to have no chose but to use fellow Sage and only the most trusted of clan members that aid us from time to time when we need a little muscle.

With this present that you received from our God, we are going to be careful about how you use it. The safeguards that he put on it may fool some of the dumbest of the Dark army, but anyone with powers can notice it magical aurora. We are under strict orders not to let anyone find out about it, and that is exactly what we are going to do. If this time devise of yours there winds up in the wrong hands, well I do not have to go any further, for you know what is at stake. While you take it on your rescue mission, I will stay here prepping a new home for the time device so now one finds it after this is all over. I think the old caverns under the Forest will do just finely, but I will have to put in a magical security system. Now leave me Night Sage for you have a lot of planning, and I must produce a list of Sage that will be following you on your trip that can be trusted.

I think we will have some long nights before us so you should go now, good night good friend and good luck. Linda went straight to her rooms to figure out who among the protectors of the Forest, as they were terms many cycles ago in the last war. She would need to take; only trusted warriors for there is bound to be some fighting and she needed the best to break out her friends. She did not have much need of the protectors of the Forest since the last War of the Clans, over a thousand cycles ago let us pray that they will be their best for a lot rides on this, not just saving her friends, but saving all the clans before this is all over. She could sense that this was just the beginning of an all-out war, and there is not going to be a clean end of this matter for she fears that many thousands of people from all the clans will be needed to overcome the Dark one this time.

Tree Mender and Flaawna where outside of the Forest Gods retreat, when they were jumped be a group of the Dark Lords followers, and they had no chance of winning a fight with this kind of odds. They decided to not press their luck and get killed, so they gave up to the Dark followers to fight another day.

With a short pray to their God to protect them, they went with them willingly; they turned out to be a group of mercenaries that wondered around the wastelands looking for a fight. Waiting for the Dark War that they were promised, by no other than their master the Dark One himself. Tree mender and Flaawna were not noticed as followers of the Forest God, thankfully this far out them assumed you were from one of the other clans in the area. So, they decided to be wondering fighters that got paid for their skills also, no wanting to be killed on the spot it they said who and what they were, and why they were in the first place. Linda would have to find her own way home for they are not going to be able to help her now. Tree Mender and Flaawna were able to convince to group of rabble-rousers that they were who they said they were for now. They had to do some fast talking, well Tree Mender did all the talking for animals do not talk, not that Flaawna wanted to talk to the likes of these.

They both figured that the less Flaawna showed what she was the better the chance of her getting out of this alive. It is a good thing in at least this moment that Scarlet Horned Netters are rare for if they were not, she would be skinned by now. So, the less attention drawn to her the better, for now she will pretend that she is what they expect her to be is his mount, but she did not like it one bit. If she got a chance to kill any one of these idiots she would in a heartbeat, but for now she had to play along and be his domesticated mount and let him ride her, how demeaning. They both decided that for now they would play along and hopefully some time down the road they could part company, for now they worked for the dark One, just until they could get out of their situation. They had to get a note to Linda and not get caught doing it, then somehow, they had to leave a trail for her to follow but how?

They decided that Flaawna would be the one to leave a trail for their rescuers for who is going to stop a large cat from doing its business in the woods it seemed only natural choice.

The first time she wondered off it was questioned but once explained no one said anything for all animals must relieve themselves. They have been double agents for over three days now and they are getting farther and farther from the point that they were picked up by the Forest God's crater. Flaawna was still leaving a trail for Linda and the rest of their rescuers but they did not know how much longer they could pull this charade off. Without raising an alarm, they were able to fit in well, but how hard is it to act like a blood thirsty buffoon looking for his next big score. It has been over a week now, they had hoped that they would be rescued in a couple of days, the problem is they keep picking up fighters along the way and now only an army could free them.

It looks as thou they may be trapped where they are for now, until they think of a plan to break out of their growing gang themselves. The only hope that they had for now was that some way Linda the Night Sage could get an army amassed to fight off this rowdy group of the Dark Lords Army, that by their accounting is growing larger each day. All they could do for now was to wait for the right chance to escape on their own. Until then they would do what they could to pass on any information they could about their situation and how many soldiers were amassing for the Dark Lord's Army.

Daphne was practicing her Mind Bump as she called it, more each day and she was getting more proficient every day, but she had hoped they had left already but the Intel coming from their area was not good. They found out about a Dark Army that was marching across the plains and was heading toward the Dark Lords prison and had plans to help break him out. So, the search for her friend Tree Mender was going to have to wait until this army is dealt with. The word coming from our supporters was that the Dark Army would eventually becoming their direction, and so they had to gather as much of the Forest Guard as they could. In the short amount of time they had left it was a large task for there are only so many of the old Guard left, they were not used since the Clan Wars. We only have a small part of them left in our service for who needs thousands of soldiers just lying around doing nothing. We had to cut down to a small piece time group of guards mostly for ceremonial purposes not real fighters, we had no need. Everything had gone so well over the last thousand cycles that most armies were disbanded permanently in all the Clans they just were not needed in time of piece. No one wanted to remember all the loss and the destruction that happened during the Clan Wars and holding on to large Armies reminded people of the troubled times so off they went without any fanfare of any kind. Now a day we do not even consider ourselves part of one clan or the other, we all just lived in piece up to a little while ago.

Most people that are under a hundred cycles do not know any more than what they are taught in schools. A war that lasted one thousand cycles cannot be summed up in the small amount of time that is given at shifting school. So, most of the younger generation has lived in nothing but piece, some do not even remember what the war was fought for. The piece that lasted so long is going to be shattered if the Sage and the

Forest Guard cannot stop the opposing army that is marching to the prison of the most dangerous God ever to live. The only thing that can stop them is the magical locks that the forest God attached to the prison when he put him there.

"Linda the Sage" as the Forest God likes to call her, was working hard at finding a peaceful way of dealing with a God that does not wish to be in the prison that he is in. She was in contact with her God as often as she could allow herself with war at her door. The Forest God was working on a way of keeping the Dark one in the cage he built over a thousand cycles ago, to a God this is but a blink of an eye, to humans it was not long enough. The Dark One was somehow breaking the locks of his prison that was supposed to keep him there for eternity. This was not an easy thing for each lock had a serious of smaller locks that could only by removed by magic. They should have been able to handle anything an evil God could think of, it did take him a thousand cycles to get to the point where he is. As far as anyone could determine that there are several locks broken which is the way he is able to influence the people outside of his prison, which can only be reached by a God for it is in the center of the world of Wardaratia. So not only did he figure out a way to break off his locks, but also how to raise it toward to surface a little at a time. The Dark One is using a massive amount of energy and magic each day to keep his followers in his control. As well the amount he is using on the locks of his prison that he called home for such a long time, for his plan to work he must control all that power without losing any of his power himself. For even a Dark God has limits to the amount of power he can take in, before becoming critical and losing all his powers forever.

This is the last thing a God wants is to lose his powers and becoming mortal and dying the way mortals do. But the Dark Lord was willing to do just that if he could not escape from the cage that has imprisoned him all these cycles. He has a plan to not only release himself from his prison, but to also defeat the ones who put him in it, especially that human who calls herself "the Night Sage."

The Sage have in these dark times have Scouts to gather intelligence as to how things are going outside their sanctuary of their Forest, and the Scouts have not been bringing back good news. One scout swore that he saw Tree Mender in the Army of the Dark Lord, and not as a captive but one of the Thousands of Mercenaries that are marching in the direction of the Forest. This raised many questions like, is he now a traitor? And if he really is part of the Dark Army, did he give away all our secrets? Is he helping them at his own accord? Or was he taken captive and is gathering information on the Mercenaries that are marching this way?

Either way it was not good news as for as Linda the Night Sage and Daphne were concerned. There is no way they can gather enough forces to be able to rescue him from the Dark Ones Army without a massive

Army of their own. Mother what are we going to do there is no way we can raise an Army to recover one person that may not want to be rescued? Daphne had tears in her eyes for she had known Tree Mender most of her life and there is no way she can believe he is a trader.

Daphne, I feel the same way as you do there is no way that he would willingly help the Dark Lord. There must be a way of finding out if he is trying to get out of a bad spot? Or if he is under the Dark Ones spell?

There are many reasons that he is with the Mercenaries for that evil horde that is marching this way. Daphne you see as I am one of the Council Members this will be addressed in a closed session to decide formally whether Tree Mender is to be cast out. Never allowed in our Forest City ever again, of course I will try to keep the council from doing anything rash.

We do not know for sure what is really happening in the camp of the Dark Lord. If we could get close enough for you to use that Mind bump trick of yours, we may be able to help him out of this mess. There is a way to get close to him without being seen, but you cannot ask me any questions about how we get there or how it works

You are in Sage training and that means you are to keep the Sage's business the Sage's do you understand what I am saying? No mother I do not but I realize that sometimes in life you may not understand why, but you know you must. There are things that we do that no one outside the sage can know about Daughter they are best left unsolicited. We are keepers of many items that cannot become the knowledge of any one outside of the Sage, for if they fall in the wrong hands, it could be detrimental to all our lives. If it got out that we have a hidden vault of items too powerful for anyone to touch. People would be breaking down the doors ordering that they either be destroyed or give them to some army to fight in some war. So, you see Daughter we protect people in many ways to they themselves do not realize every day, now back to my point. I received an item not too long ago that has powers that we will be using to try to break out Tree Mender and Flaawna if they are still alive. You cannot know any more about it, for it is one of the items that will be in the vault when we are successful in our mission. Now it looks as thou because of the danger involved that you and I are the only ones to go to rescue our friends. Now go pack enough cloths for a quick trip we will be leaving in three quarters of solar cycle. There is a way to get close to him without being seen, but you cannot ask me any questions about how we get there or how it works. I will call for you when I am ready to leave now go and prepare for our trip, I need to wrap up some things, but I should be done in time. As Linda she did not have many responsibilities, but she is also Linda the Night Sage she had many duties and she could not leave without informing the High Sage Gretta about her plans. So, if something goes wrong, well you get what I am trying to say, now back to my Sage duties so I can leave on time.

When I approached Gretta with my plans, she was alarmed that we were going without any kind of escort. Then I told her how we planned to use the time devise and she felt better about it all and wished us a safe trip. We may need a couple of specialty items that if I get caught, I will have a lot of explaining to do, "why did I not go through the proper channels" and stuff like that. I do not want to go into too much detail about my plans, but I know that this rescue is going to be dicey. I am running out of time to get all that we need for this trip, if we cannot get both Tree Mender and Flaawna then I will have to leave one behind.

There will be to many solders around and if Tree Mender does not get away, he will have to produce a story as to what happened so he can try to save his Ass. I got most of the items that I needed and had one quarter of a solar cycle left which should be enough time if I do not get caught. There was a Sage in front of the vault most of the time but not today for I made the schedule and so I managed to leave a gap in the vault guard so I could sneak in without any questions. I had to time it correctly for if I were too early, I would have to answer for trying to remove items without permission. I went down to where the vault is to sneak in and get out before getting caught, and to my surprise there was still a guard at the door. Without permission from the Council members I would not stand any chance of removing the items I wanted under short notice.

What can I do to remove the items now that the guard never got the new schedule as to where she would come in a little later than normal? Wait I can test the time device that the Forest god made for the rescue of my daughter, well at least we are using it to rescue our friends. Maybe if I time it right no one will see me traveling in time to go back to normal time after.

I was about to pull out the Time Device when Gretta the High Sage came down the stairs looking right at me, "I knew I would find you down here" said Gretta. Did you not think to ask me to secure the items for your trip, for if you planed on using a certain object on a Sage member you would have many questions to answer for? Now leave this up to me I will meet you outside of my office, do you have a list of items that you need for your trip or were you just planning to clean out the whole vault.

I handed her the list of items that I wanted to use on the rescue, her eyes went wide when she saw what was on my list, and then they went cold. If you were not going up against an army I would have to say no, but you are going up against the Dark Lords army, so I will get the items in question for you. One of us if not both of us will have to answer to the Council if this gets out, so you had better come back successful. If all of this is in vain then heads will roll, and I think you can tell who they will be now go I will meet you outside of my office. I will call Daphne and ask her to meet you there, "you will call her?" How can that be possible? Linda said why do you question me daughter for all the time you were talking with a God. Daphne taught me how to use her "Mind Bump" now go before I change my mind and not let you go on this journey of yours. As Linda the Night Sage got to the High Sages office, she indeed found her daughter Daphne before her. Hello Daughter, I see that your Mind Bump worked, and Gretta got thru to you, for here you are. You are going to have to teach me how to do it before your new way to communicate catches on and I am the only one that does not know how to do it. Daphne chuckled at that and said she would teach me as soon as possible and then she laughed some more, only to be stopped by the approach of the High Sage Gretta.

Here are the items that you wanted and do I have to tell you of the ramifications if you do not return with every one of them, Yes I understand and thank you for your sticking your neck out on the line to help us.

Daphne took the items from the Gretta and carefully put them in a pack for she had no idea what any of the items where for, but she did not want to set anything off and give away their plans. They loaded up everything in their packs and said their goodbyes to Gretta along with one more thank you they were on their way.

Once past the gates to their Forest they started in the direction of where Tree Mender and Flaawna were last seen. After about a quarter of a solar cycle they stopped, so Linda could remove the one item that will save them the most time. Linda pulled out the item that looked like an old piece of junk, until she investigated it while concentrating, she focused her inner magic to activate it. Then you could see the beauty of the object in her hands and it looked like anything other than junk, it was bright and shiny with gems shimmering all over it. Hold on to my hand or you will be left behind, and I am sure you do not want to miss this, Daphne grabbed on to her mother's arm and with a flash they were off.

The Forest God had informed her to be careful as to where she picks as her landing spot, so she did not wind up standing in the middle of a group of angry hordes of solders. They did not expect to land in the exact location they were in and they did just what they were not to do.

Linda put her hand over Daphne's mouth for they landed right in front of the Dark Lord's men. They appeared in a small area of shrubs not ten feet from a cluster of solders about to eat. Linda wished that she had taken the time to learn Daphne's Mind Bump for it could come in handy right about now, that is when she felt a kick to her leg. She forgot that her hand was over her daughter's nose and mouth, and Daphne could not breathe and that was the reason for the kick. They knew that they were in a bad predicament and they had to think fast to get out of it, her mother made a sign of a small insect. And that we should shift into a small insect and get out of here.

Wow that was twice now that beginning shifting 101 got her out of a tight jam, what are the odds of that really working outside of school. Once Daphne came to grips with the severity of their situation she shifted into a small bug and they got out of there. After a long time scurrying about on the littlest legs that she ever thought would save her butt they came to a stop. They were now far enough away to shift back to their own self's and gather their wits. They were in a small bush further then the last and now could get a good look without getting caught, Linda asked "are you ok." "Yes" came the reply, for they were both winded from crawling about on such small legs and not getting far. Now that they were ok, Linda asked Daphne to try a mind bump for Tree Mender to see if he was nearby. I will try but if he is not with the group of solders that we ran away from I may not be able to reach him. Daphne focused the power in her so she could project her mind out word to see if she could notice anyone that she knew. She explained it to her mother but Linda the Night Sage by night and mother by day did not think she could achieve much without much more practice. As Daphne searched the area nearby with her mind, she could not reach out to him without knowing for sure or they could get one of the dark Lords men. She moved her mind out further to hear for the minds near and far for the one that she knew well. Tree Mender was up all night on lookout duty and was sleeping at the time Daphne found his mind and Bumped him in his sleep. He was in a makeshift barracks so when he jumped up from the "Bump" from Daphne, at first, he did not understand what was happening and had to cover up his response. He looked around ant noticed several solders that were wakened by the ruckus and had to produce some story as to why he woke up half the barracks. Daphne "Bumped" him again cautiously to make sure she had to right mind, and the voice that she heard in her mind was defiantly was no mistake it was Tree Mender.

She told him that they were somewhere nearby but if he could try to escape from his would-be captors; if he got caught, they would not think twice about killing him on the spot. He made up a story about needing to relieve himself and stepped out to talk to Daphne without causing a stir. Tree Mender could have attracted a crowd if he did not leave for a walk in the woods; for he did not yet understand the way to talk to her was with his mind not his mouth. With a chuckle Daphne went on to explain how the "mind bump" worked and to his embarrassment he finally figured out that she was in his mind and that he did not need to move his mouth to talk. Tree Mender went on to say how much he was glad to hear her voice even if it was from a distance and not around him. He went on to explain how he had wound up in the service of the Dark Lord and his mercenary army. That is as you know, on the march right to them and had orders to destroy the forest that they all held dear, and just so you know Flaawna was ok and she was healthy for now. Daphne stopped him from rambling about for he was so glad that he was about being rescued from the hell that the Dark Army was. They have no feeling about anything, but go about destroying everything in their path, it took everything he had in him to not kill them all. He was never a person quick to anger, but you just do not cull a group of trees by the thousands for War Machines and not make him mad. Daphne understood how he felt for she had seen him work on many sick and dying trees and tenderly coax the trees back to good health. He had a tender heart and to hear him talk of killing someone bothered her, for if he killed someone, he lost his shifting powers. All his magic to care for the trees that he loved so would be gone for good and that would destroy him for caring for the trees was his life. They did not have much time before he would be missed so they got to the point How they were going to break him out and not bring down the whole Dark Army down around their head? They had to get him out of there, so he did not get himself captured or worse having to kill someone, trying to gain his freedom.

They decided to wait until it was a night with no moons, so it would be dark enough for them to try to free him, which meant him staying there a couple of days. For the weather was getting colder so the Winter cycle was near, which meant dark cold nights. For now, we were in contact with tree Mender and know he is safe for the moment, they can always break him out quicker if they had to, but they could not have any bloodshed. Tree Mender understood that they had to wait but he could not help but smile for he was going to be out of this nightmare soon. He needed to be careful about being to giddy or he could be questioned about his new demeanor, so he went back into the character that he had been the whole time in the army of the dammed. Tree Mender was helping in the camp kitchen and was doing his best not to be noticed, he had to think fast when he was asked by a solder as to what his name was. He had to think quickly as to what he should be called, he produced Johnny Long sword to give the appearance that he would fit in and not get killed on the spot. He felt bad that he was miss leading some of the people that he came to know that he cooked with, for they were just like him, in the wrong place at the time. So, as it came to be that I was Johnny of the cook's guild and was sent to work with the others that they noticed the way. He went back to his duties in the kitchens scrubbing pot after pot after each meal, for they all had to be cleaned before he could eat himself. So, if you were hungry you had better work fast, so you have a little time to eat before the days next meal had to be cooked. Being in the cook's guild saved him from having to kill anyone that got in the way just for looking at you wrong. For the Dark Lord was ruthless and so his followers were just as ruthless and killed without any care about whom or what it was. The Dark Lord was to repay his faithful followers when he was freed and after they killed anyone that helped putting him there.

Tree Mender got ill the first time he saw the brutality of the Dark Ones followers and had to produce a story about him being sick with the flu. That was a narrow escape, and after that he tried to stay as far back in the Dark hoard as possible so as not to have a repeat of that again. He was so horrified by the carnage that was all around him, for not only did they kill everyone but also every living thing. Weather it was used to feed the army or out of meanness it did not matter for they had blood lust in their eyes and only more blood could satisfy it. There trusted for they were addicted to the feeling that they felt when they killed and needed to kill over and over to feed their addiction. They were all in the grip of the evil that the Dark Lord dished out to his pleasure for he received more power and more control over his henchmen with every evil act. It was bad now but if they did not find a way to keep the Dark Lord locked up and his mouth quieted so he could no longer influence any Clan Members. For there was to be no piece in the lands if he got his way with his evil plans our people would be lost, I fear.

Gretta of the High Sage was worried to death over the fact that she let Daphne and her mother Linda go on a rescue mission without any solders to protect them if something went wrong. She blamed herself for not insisting that they took more people, they were overdue now and she was getting worried that something may have happened to them all.

What was she going to tell the High Council if they did not return and the items that that removed from the vault got in the hands of the Dark One? What could have gone wrong? Why did they not try to reach out to her threw Daphne's Mind Bump thing? No, she was just being silly old women, but she could not help herself, she prayed to the Forest God daily asking him to keep his hand over them and protect them. People were starting to ask questions about their absence, and she was finding it harder with each daily cycle of the suns to appease all the questions going around.

Thank the Forest God that she was the highest-ranking Sage and no one dear question her word, if she said something it was good as the law.

But soon she may be called before the Council as to whether she knew of where they went and why she had covered up to whole thing. God help me if they found out she helped them remove items from the vault without going to the Council for approval. She was so worried for them all and prayed that they would return safely and do it soon so this would all be over. Gretta was the High Sage and as a priestess of the Forest God and as High Sage she could lose everything over one rash decision for she was to appear a certain way for her people to look upon her as pure in all things. What is keeping them? She thought as her mind wandered as she hoped they did not get captured or killed.

Linda the Night Sage was keeping busy while they waited for the right time to spring Tree Mender and Flaawna, she was listening in the camp threw her shifting powers. She shifted into a firebird one for they were plentiful in these parts and they had great vision to see from a distance.

As well as some small slime worms which was perfect for, she came and went without being noticed. They all were getting more worried by the day for they did not wish to stay in one place to long so the guards would not find them. Daphne was in touch with Johnny aka Tree Bender several times a day and he could get caught sneaking around instead of doing his chores in the cook's kitchens. He and I were both getting the much-needed practice at Mind Bumping each other and we were working on the distance. So that they could communicate in case they had to move further back from the Mercenaries camp they had to be careful, so they did not get caught. The Mercenaries were camped in the same place as we found them, and it seemed as thou they were waiting for something or someone. They finally got the break that they were hoping for the past couple of days, the word came down that they were to resume their advance toward the Forest God's people. With all the commotion of the camp moving out it would be easier for them to spring Tree Mender from his trap in the Dark Lords army. They decided that just before the extensive line of the army where to advance they could free him without too much trouble, at least they hoped. They went over the plan in their minds threw the Mind Bump of Daphne's powers that she taught to them, it was about time and some big guy walked up to "Johnny." And he said, "that he was needed in the front of the mercenaries hoard and that a commander of the guard wanted to talk to him." This could not be good for he was never called upon by anyone in the Dark Lord's army let alone one of the commanders wanting to see him this could not be good.

He was escorted to a tent that said that a commander Wolfslog oversaw this area of the army and his rank, Johnny was told to wait in front until he was called in. Oh! God of the forest what had I done now? Could they have found out about my escape plans? He was about to run for his life when a guard standing at the tents front door was to escort him in now, God help me please. The Commander called General Wolfslog called for him to sit down in the open chair in front of his desk, so I am informed that you have a large battle Cat. What was he talking about?

He must be talking about Flaawna, why yes sir I do have a large cat that I raised up from a youngster. I call her Flaawna, but I do not own her for she is loyal to me, but she is still very wild, she will not let most people near her. Especially when she is hungry and wishes to hunt, she goes off without any care and stays gone for up to a week. What is your name?

For I was informed that you worked in the kitchens, but no one knew your name not even the people that worked with you. Excuse me for not telling you sooner, my name is Johnny Long Sword sir, but that is just a name that I wish not to remember. For my father's name was the first Long Sword in a lengthy line of cooks until he disgraced our family name when he and a small group of drunkards ravaged a small fishing village and slaughtered everyone including the smallest of children sir.

So you see our family was now looked upon as outlaws and hunted until they killed every one in my family, sparing me because I was a small child and they spared my life but my family name was blackened from that day on. I could leave the village that up to that point was my home by I was banished from that day on, so I changes my name so to have a chance in the world. That is a sad story, but I was more interested about that Cat of yours, what is it called? Oh yes "Flaawna" her name will have to be changed if I plan to ride it into battle. You will be the one to make that animal of yours into the battle cat that I wish, or you and the cat will be killed, you may go now. I will expect you both back here early in the morning after the army marches off, we will stay behind until I am able to ride that cat into battle or until you are dead, now leave me. Tree Mender could not believe what had just happened, if he did not make Flaawna into a Battle Cat in a truly short amount of time they would both be killed on the spot. If he did get Flaawna to go along with the General's request then Flaawna could be killed in battle, or worse someone may recognize him as a Scarlet Horned Netter, and he would for sure die. He was as confused as what just happened. He did not dare even think of making a beautiful animal, even one of the last of his species into the monster that was wanted out of him. Not that he could any way, for Flaawna would rather eat him then going along with a half-baked scheme that all he had to do is run away and to her the problem would be solved. But where would that put him, for not doing as an officer asked would for sure. Daphne was outraged by what she heard, for she was listening in to the conversation threw the Mind Bump, and she let him know in flat terms that there was no way he was training Flaawna for her death. There had to be another way out of this that they could all get away and still has their freedom when everything was over. They had to talk to her mother Linda and find out if there is anything from the vault that can get them out of this mess, all she knew was she was not telling Flaawna about the General's plan for her.

Chapter VII

When Linda the Night Sage was informed of what the General's orders for him and Flaawna were, she could not believe what she was hearing. Why had their God allowed this to happen to them? The main thing now was to somehow produce a new plan before tomorrow's deadline. Then it came to her, that with no one around it would be easier for them to get out of there, they just needed the right plan. They all agreed that this could be the only way to gain their friends freedom; they could not kill anyone that was out of the question, even our she cats Flaawna. They needed to all be in the same place so they can plan their escape without anyone getting hurt or killed. Linda was a Sage and, on the Council, how would it sound if she ordered or even let someone kill for her? Or for her daughter who is a Sage in training. At the very least they could get out of this with their hides, on that is, but that was not going too happened. For Linda planed for something like this and brought all kinds of "goodies," if they had to use the items that she brought with that would not be the best plan but so be it. It would be a shame to go back without using at least some of the vault items even if she did get in trouble with the Council. They decided to meet just before the General was to expect "Johnny Long Sword" and his pacified Battle Cat in training, as Flaawna was to be called. At least for now until the General picked a more suitable name for his Battle Cat. He was going to ride into Battle on his prized stead, just think if somebody recognized Flaawna as a Scarlet Horned Netter. He might have a revolt on his hands over such a prized animal that is slaughtered for its magical fur. That would be nice if the General's men killed him for the mount that he so prized, but not for its power but for his vanity. While all the mercenary army ran around getting the camp broke down "Johnny" as he is called in camp, sat in a secluded spot to talk to Flaawna about the Generals plan. And how are they going to stay behind to train so that the General could make you into his Battle Cat that he can ride into war?

The more Tree Mender talked the more Flaawna got upset at the idea of some arrogant general wanting to force her into being his War Cat. By the end of the story with what happened and how they were to stay, the more Flaawna wanted to rip out this General's throat. She asked if she could just wander off and not come back that would fix the Generals plans would not it, but then you are left behind to take the wrath of this blow hard. Wait a minute we have been talking with Daphne and Linda about a plan they must spring us from this Hell Hole. We do not have all the details together yet, but this will be our only hope to escape if it does not get us killed in the process.

Linda the Night Sage was looking at the items that she removed from the vault to see what she could use to break out her friends from the trap they were in. Let see I have not seen some of the items since the Clan Wars over a thousand years ago. After going thru the items, she found the perfect item for their situation, it is an item that was the favorite of a long dead Magic user called The Snake Handler. The item makes it appear as thou there are thousands of deadly snakes all around you. And if they bit you your mind thinking that the snakes are real causes a heart attack and you die on the spot. The mind is a very fragile part of your body. You can be hallucinating due to a powerful herb or spell and your mind will see it as a real event you can die from the power of your own mind. For what you see may not be real, but you still can die from it if your mind thinks it is so. Now all they had to do is plan how and when they were going to release the snakes and hope the General gets scared enough, for us to break in and out without any complications. The spell was so effective in the Clan Wars that up until the death of The Snake Handler he caused over a thousand people to death in the Clan Wars right up until his own spell killed him. He was casting spell after spell when his mind got distracted by a soldier from one of the enemy lines coming towards him.

He Caused him to lose control of his spell and fell prey to his own magic, the soldier picked up his Snake Wand and it eventually wound up in the hands of the Sage. We had the start of a plan, but what if the snakes do not get the desired effect? We needed a backup plan, so we do not get worse off than we are in the first place. If there are any guards left behind our plan would be finished before we had started, but what else could we use that was powerful enough if the first plan failed? We could use the Time Devise that the God of the Forest fashioned with his own hands. But if anyone saw it, we could be worse off for we were told that no one could see it. It could bring down all kinds of ramifications with time even causing a rift that could change time. Worse we could change the natural course of events, besides all that we would have an angry God also. The thing with magical items many times they would do more harm than they did well. In the time of the Clan Wars that was not thought about much. They did not care about anything but death destruction and to everyone and anything. The Forest God was busy working out plans of his own as to how he was going to put a stop to the Dark One, who was getting more powerful each day. At this rate, the Dark Lord will be free from the cell that he was in for over a thousand year in no time at all. He could be leading his army against the Forest God and his people in a matter of weeks or months, it was hard to tell at the point.

One thing that he did know was that somehow, he had to fix the locks that he worked on so hard to keep the Dark God in his prison and it had to be fixed soon. He was working around the clock to produce new locks to replace the ones that were broken and to find a way to seal off the Dark One forever. Being a God did not mean that you possessed infinite powers that you could tap into at will, even God is had limits. The limits are much more than your average person, but once those limits are met, he had to recover and build up his powers over time.

At this rate he was going to need plenty of time to recover and while he is doing that the Dark One will be free to do as he wished. His powers were dwindling but he had to stop the plans of the dark army with their plans to destroy anything in their path. He had to find help from the other Gods, for they will be the next on the Dark Ones hit list after he is finished off, there was no way he could do it on his own. The "Dark Lord" as he is called now also has the same limitations as we but has have a thousand cycles to grind away at his prison. He also can drain his followers of their power so he can feed off them, thus gaining more power. The Dark Lord does not care who he kills and will drain the power of all his followers until they die off, a shell of what they use to be. The other God's have not gotten along due to their needs to be the most powerful, jealousy among the other God's caused a rift between them and they each went their own way. They each claimed a different element to live in and people to worship them, they were the Land, Sea, Earth, and Sky each claiming the four corners of the planet back then called Wardar. Over time each God grew more secluded and vowed to never speak to each other ever again for their jealousy grew that much.

The other God's never were seen again after that, and they may not be alive anymore, for all he knew, yes Gods live for an exceptionally long time, but they are mortal. They stay alive if there are people to worship them, the more people to believe in them the more powers they have. If one of the four clans died off their God would lose all his strength and slowly over time die off. Of course, the opposite is true as well the more people that worship them the more ability, they had to help their people in a time of need. Being the biggest and the most powerful all depends on the people that worship you, for just like any God they are only as powerful as their people. The dark One is feeding off his followers and the more they grow in number the more power he receives, soon he will grow too powerful to stop.

Back in the forest, the Sage had started to listen to the rumors that people were talking about. Is Tree Mender a spy for the Dark One? Is he part of his dark army? If he is, will he lead the Dark Hoard here to their very doorstep? These were just some of the rumors that were being told in the open markets that were making the people of the Forest God question if the Sage were doing enough to protect them. The High Sage herself was under scrutiny by the council, for what happened the night that a fellow Sage may have left to join the Dark Army with items long thought gone. Gretta was trying to keep everything under control while Daphne and her mother Linda the Night Sage that were past due on their rescue mission, and with every lunar cycle that past it was harder to deflect questions as to her ware about. Gretta The High Sage was starting to wish she had gone with Linda and Daphne, so she did not have to answer all the questions of where they are. She was in hot water with the Council over what may or may not of happened the night Linda the Night Sage left without informing the council of her plans. There were even rumors of Linda being removed for her seat and her title if she were found a treasonous spy for the Dark Lord,

God knows what she could tell them about their forest compound. Linda and all the others needed to return soon before they are tried and found guilty without them even here to defend themselves. Gretta had more pressing matters to worry about, the Dark Army is heading this way and if not stopped ahead of time they will be at our door in no time. With the Army that is amassing for the Dark One, they will never stand a chance without intervention; everyone that could swing a weapon was needed to defend the Forest. The rest were in the temple praying for the Forest God to help them out of the mess that was heading their way. With all the turmoil in the forest, the Sage were busy handling people's questions like, "What do you plan on doing to protect us?"

Some of the Sage combing thru the records of the Clan Wars to see if there were any answers as what was done back then that could help them now, but with little luck. Every one of the Sage were busy with one thing or another, even the Sage in training were being put to work answering all the questions that were pouring in. Some were even wondering if their God were doing enough to protect them, which was the worst thing that could happen. They needed to pull together more now than ever to pull around their God and ask for his strength. The council members called for a special meeting to discuss what to do about the War that was marching right to their front door. The entire council members had to be there for a mandatory meeting to deal with several pertinent questions that the council now wanted answers for. One of the questions they wanted to address was the disappearance of several key members of the Forest, and what is to be done to insure their save return. That is if the rumors were false then they will deal with searching for them, If the rumors are true than they had a problem as to they are traders and working for the Dark Lord. Then they will be tried for treason and their fate with be up to a Forest Court. The Forest Court has not convened for over a hundred cycles, for there is no crime in the forest and has not had any crimes since the time of the Clan Wars. Gretta as the highest Sage member and usually sat in the head chair and led the council, but she is to be questioned today. About the night Linda the Night Sage left the forest to join Tree Mender in the Dark Army.

With her judgment in question today she is to be seated in the front of the council waiting for them to question her. Her actions of that day will be in question as to whether she gave Linda the Night Sage items of

Magical properties to aid the Dark Army. The council was normally not in session unless there was a problem that needed to be dealt with, that could not be solved with conventional ways. She could only pray that something would happen before the council asked her questions about the night Linda left. She prayed to the Forest God for help in her time of need.

Linda was getting tired of waiting for the Dark Army to gather up their camp, so she shifted into a very small bug and went over to the Dark Lords Army to see what she could find. She told Daphne to wait there and keep her eyes open and if she sees is anyone to shift into something and get out of there. Linda crawled over to where the General's tent was and decided to see what she could glean for his tent about Johnny aka Tree Mender. She saw the General was not alone and she so wanted to find out what he was talking about that she crawled over to his desk without thinking about it. The General was talking to a solder about his plan of staying behind and that the solder was to take command of the Army while he was absence. He told the solder that he would meet up with the rest of the Army in a couple of weeks. And that they were to march about one solar week and then set up camp and wait for him to return. Linda also heard the complaints from the solder about leaving him along, and what if something happened that he should leave behind a couple of guards for his safety. At that point, the General got mad, for the solder was not following his orders and questioning his ability to lead without needing a babysitter. He yelled at the soldier to do what he was told and not to question his authority, or he could be replaced. The solder was shocked by the General's strong feelings on the matter and apologized for questioning him. He was then dismissed and told to carry out his orders and to lead the Army to the place he spoke of and wait for him to arrive.

Linda chooses this time to exit the tent as well and tell her friend what she overheard. She scurried back the way she came so as not to draw attention to her. But with her tiny legs she was not making very much progress and at this pace it could take her quite a while.

She was able to communicate with Daphne threw the Mind Bump that her daughter produced, and what will be called "new magic." She will have to tell her how proud of her she is, when this is all over with but now, she needed to focus on the problem at hand. She contacted her daughter's mind and informed her of what she overheard and that they would need to act fast, or they may lose this opportunity. When she reached the area that she left her daughter she was surprised with what she saw standing there in her place was a "God" in all his glory. She had never seen this God, but he was dressed he could only be the God of the Water Clan for she had seen drawings of him when she was very little.

The God before her was Orcefious the God of the Water Clan was staring down at her looking a little put out over the wait he had for her return. She was a Sage and it was her life's choice to serve the God of the Forest, but she had never met any other of the Gods of the Clans. She did not know what the proper protocol was, so she just introduced herself hoping not to insult him in any way, for he was a minor God But still processed much power. That which she did not want to be used on her on her in any way, so she gave him the same respect that she did her God. She waited quietly for the God before her to speak, for she could feel the power coming from him and gave him the respect that he was used to commanding. Orcefious sat on a nearby rock and looked as though he was in his own watery Court; he called for me to approach him for he had some questions that she needed to answer.

She approached him and asked how she could help him? He wasted no time and explained why he came to her on this day to answer the questions that she could answer. He knew of her meetings with the Forest God and her aiding him in the capture of the Dark Lord, and came to her to ask about the Forest God, for he requested a meeting of the Gods and that was never done before.

As a God you are weary of the other God's and expect them to stay in their own corner of the world. Gods are not used to serving anyone for it is the other way around that they are served by their followers and did not jump to any Gods whim no matter how powerful he may be. The Water God then looked as though he was hit by an arrow; he looked scared for just a minute, then he asked about the plans of her God to do away with the Dark One for good. She gave him the information that she knew and gave her opinion as to their chances on defeating the Dark Lord. She did not think it could be done without help, for he is much stronger this time. She did not know if that was the answer that he wanted for the Water God left soon after she gave him her opinion.

Linda the Night Sage hoped that this was not going to be the story for the other God's as to visit at any whim. She did not need to be known as a listening post for any other God. She only knew one God and as a servant to the Forest God that was good enough for her, she did not wish to be an ear to the God's. Linda needed to find where her daughter went to and get out of this jam before anything else popped up. She did not know what her God was up to but if he is calling for a meeting of the Gods then he must have a plan. Now back to the problem at hand, how was she going to free Tree Mender and Flaawna without bringing down the whole Dark Army? She searched for her daughter, in her Mind eye to find her faster than looking for her by foot. That is when she saw the events that happened while she was gone. She saw her daughter in the woods looking for berries and other plants they were eatable. Then she saw all the solders marching her direction about to overcome her, but she had her back to them, so she did not see them until it was too late.

Linda wished that she had never left to see what was going on with the General, for if she did not, she would have been able to see the trouble that her daughter was in before this.

She wanted to scream a warning, but it was too late, for this scene already played out and was but a vision of what happened earlier. She had no idea what happened to her daughter Daphne, but she had to find her fast and get out of here before anything else happened. She refused to wait any longer she decided that she will use to Time Devise to free everyone and worry about the ramifications later. She did not know where Daphne was, but she did know where Tree Mender was and if she moved quickly, she may be able to rescue everyone at the same time.

Hopefully, Daphne got away from the guards that were about to overtake her position and she was not looking around to see if anyone was coming. Oh well if she did get captured, she knew where she would wind up this may just work out. Linda decided that there was no time to waste so she reached into her bag to get the Time Devise and pulled out an ugly looking rock. With her powers focused on what she wanted she saw the rock turn into a beautiful gold item with gears moving about.

Linda the Night Sage thought where she wanted to be and was wiped off to the camp of the Dark Lord. She needed to be quick to get everyone out without anyone seeing her, the Time Devise worked in several ways, and she could speed up time so that no one can see her. Or she can slow down very slow and everyone would be trapped in time while she moved around in a Time Bubble. Linda moved thru time at a faster rate than the people around her making her invisible in the slowed down time of the camp. Linda had to get use to moving around such a fast pace, it only took her a couple of minutes to figure out how the Time Devise worked. So, with her practice complete she sped off toward where she last saw Tree Mender and Flaawna so she could speed them back to the forest and then she needed to find Daphne. Linda was able to find Flaawna right away, so she ran over to her and with the both in the Time Bubble they were able to flee threw time without anyone noticing.

They stopped in a clearing just outside of the forest where they decided it would be better to all go into the forest together so Flaawna waited for her to return. Linda raced back to get Tree Mender and did not see him in the kitchens so she looked around the Mercenary camp and to the people around her they would only feel a slight breeze. She looked all over the camp and found Tree Mender in the tent of the General, and the General did not look happy. She wanted to slow time down just a little to find out what he was saying but thought better of it. By the look on the General's face he was questioning Tree Mender about his Battle Cat disappearing. So, with no time to tell Tree Mender what she was about to do she grabbed him up and ran thru time to the spot she left Flaawna.

When she slowed down to deposit him in the clearing Tree Mender was terribly upset for, he did not understand what Linda did. What just happened? One minute he was being yelled at about Flaawna disappearing, and then he was dropped by some force that he could not feel or see. I was like it was a blink in time that propelled him to this place. When he settled down, he noticed that he and Flaawna were both brought to the same place. Flaawna will you please tell Tree Mender what had just happened I have to find my daughter, pray to the God of the Forest that she is ok. Linda the Night Sage went back in the Time Bubble to go back to the last place she saw her daughter in a clearing near the camp. She called out to Daphne threw the Mind Bump her daughter taught her and received no response back. Either Daphne was not in the area or her mind was being blocked somehow, no matter what it was Linda the Night Sage was not leaving without her daughter. Linda went up to the camp to find out what she could from the solders and to find the solders that may have taken her daughter. She used the Time Bubble once more to look around the camp without the chance of getting caught herself. Since to last time she spirited away with Tree Mender the camp was different, for everyone was scrambling about looking for the attackers that took two members of their army.

Linda continued to look about the camp for any sign of her daughter, and the men she saw about to overtake her in the clearing near the camp. Without any luck she went into the General's tent to see if she could glean anything about Daphne, what she found inside the tent rocked her to the very core of her being. Before her was a beast that she thought was long deceased the ugly beast that was in the General's tent was last seen in the thousand-year Clan Wars. How could it be that this evil beast from the depths of evil long lost somehow it was in the tent in front of her. This beast was able to detect magic no matter how little there was, she dear not get any closer, for the beast not only detect magic, but it also drained the individual of their magic forever. She had to tell the Council about what she just saw. Pray that it was not able to trace the magic in the Time Devise for it could go after a God just as well as any other magical creature. The hunt for Daphne would have to wait, for if there is one creature from the Clan Wars there could be others as well. If the Dark Horde had creatures of the Clan Wars, what else could they be hiding? There was no telling what was already released upon their planet, she needed to hurry back to her Forest home. To have the warning sirens ring out across the land to call the Council into order so they can be told of this new turn of events and address what she learned.

Linda the Night Sage quietly left the tent as fast as she dares so not to attract the attention of the "Dissolver" as it was known a Thousand cycles ago. Linda returned to the spot where she dropped off Tree Mender and Flaawna and found them in a heated discussion about who knows what. She intervened in their conversation so she could get back to the subject that she needed to convey what she saw and to inform them about the Dissolver. Tree Mender's mouth was wide open in shock and Flaawna looked visibly scared.

Linda had never seen Flaawna scared of anything, but she is "magical" creature and would be dissolved until there was no magic left. Linda thought about it for a minute and it was not something she wanted to experience herself, for she has magical abilities and could not live her present life without magic. Magic is so much part of her daily life she would be nothing without it, for her magic is why she is where she is today. She dreaded to think what would happen if there are more than the one, she saw, the world that they knew could end, without the magic they used each day just to survive. Back to the subject at hand the only one that they can do anything about, they needed to get back to the

Forest and gather up the council members to tell them what they saw and heard. Tree Mender let Linda know about what they were discussing when she popped in. Tree Mender went to the Gates of the Forest and saw a flyer posted on a tree of all things, saying that he was to be considered a trader for joining up with the Dark Army and that Linda the Sage was also wanted for treason. Linda was shocked by what she had just heard; she could sort everything out if she could just talk to Gretta the High Sage. She decided that it may be safer it she contacted Gretta threw a Mind Bump to find out what is going on before she goes in blind. Linda had some trouble reaching Gretta for she was in the council chamber up on charges herself for aiding a potentially trader to their way of life. Gretta informed them that they needed to come to the council chambers at once and not to fight if they are taken into custody by the Forest Guard. What had been going on around here when she had been gone? Everything that she worked for was now in jeopardy if the council does not believe her. Linda had to find a way to get in the council chambers without being dragged to the jail to await trial. She had the Time Devise, but do she dare use it, she was told not to let anyone to see it, and then there was that Time Distortion this he talked about. Gretta informed her whatever her plan was that they needed to hurry before the council finds her guilty of aiding the Dark Lord.

Linda had to think about what the best way was to get into the council chambers so she can inform them about what she saw while spying on the Dark Hoard. Tree Mender said this was his entire fault for if she had not come after him none of this would have happened. This is no time for anyone pointing the finger at who was to blame, she would have done it again a hundred times over they were her friends and that is what friends do. Now they were out of time she needed to get into the council and save another friend that stuck her head out when she did not have to.

Flaawna you should spend time together here for a while until we can get this cleaned up, until then we still have no way to get into the council chambers. Linda the Night Sage called out to her friend Gretta to help them get into the council and inform them that she was on her way to explain everything. We need to go now Tree Mender and no matter what happens do not fight the guards if they try to escort us to the council.

They held hands and walked into the Forest Gates with all the pride that what they did was just, and as she expected the Guards were on them within seconds. Linda could only hope that Gretta was able to sway the council to have them brought before them at once so they can clear all of this up. Gretta the high Sage was talking with the council members that Linda and Tree Mender were on their way here, with the council's permission that is. Gretta was doing as much damage control as possible, so that they can get to the information that Linda was bringing back that was of vital importance. In came Linda and Tree Mender being marched in by the guards, the guards? Are they serious? These where respected members of the forest clan, what is going to be next? Locking them up, how has it come to this? Gretta prayed to her God that all this would come out all right and that they could get to the problems at hand dealing with the Army marching towards them.

Thankfully, Linda and Tree Mender were taken straight to the council chamber where she hoped that she could straighten out without getting into too much trouble. Linda as a Sage was asked to approach the council members to explain her actions, for the first time in her life she was a little scared of the council. With all the poise that she could muster she approached the council, where upon doing so she noticed that her friend Gretta the High Sage was not in her usual spot. This could wind up bad for all involved Linda waited for the council to ask for her to explain herself, and after a while the chairpersons spoke and read of the charges or her crimes. She could not believe it has come to this, her the Night Sage and Champion of the Forest God was standing charges for rescuing her friends. After all the charges were read, she was finally given a chance to speak in her behalf, she went down the list of events as they happened. She did her best to explain that neither she nor anyone that she rescued where never any part of the Dark Lord Army. She explained that yes, she removed some items from the vault without going thru the proper channels, but her friends needed her and there was no time to lose. For if she waited too long her friend Tree Mender could have been discovered and put to death. She explained that she removed the items from the vault, but never used them and no one knew what she possessed. She was truly sorry for not asking permission from the council, but she did so because she knew that they would not agree, and that was why she did not ask. She asked if she could tell the council what she learned while in her camp just a little way from the Dark Hoard that was marching their direction. She explained that upon being approached by a group of mercenaries Tree Mender did the only thing that he could do at the time without being killed on the spot. So, he chooses to go under cover and find out what the Hoard was up to, he at no time ever killed or told anyone his real identity. He was known as "Johnny Long Sword" and the whole time he worked in the kitchen cleaning and washing dirty pots and pans.

She reminded the council of the oath that she took as a young Sage to always tell the truth and to never disgrace the Forest God by any conduct of hers or others in her charge. She also went on to say that she saw a creature from the darkest time of the Clan Wars. It was toward the last part of the War of the Clan's when the magic users we are desperate to win the war that lasted way to long. They started to mess with very dark magic. Come to think of it; the "Black Cloud" that hovered about darkening everything, more as the war progressed grew to its darkest around this time. The evil that possessed everyone and thing, but stopped just short of our precious forest, it must of felt that the Forest God and his people were not the immense trouble that would be needed to bring us under its control. No one at the time knew that the blacker than black cloud was a very dark force that we now call the Dark Lord. Back to the Dissolver it feeds on your Magic until you are nothing more than a shell, without a tiny dust of magic. They were outcast and lived outside of any Clan for without any powers in the War you were no good to them, so out you went to fend for yourself. With no friends and no one to take them in, they started to huddle together in small groups for some protection. There were others without magic, but these were the warriors that killed in battle and they still had worth for them for they still had their strength. They lost their powers following the commands of their leader and would die for the bravely fighting to the death for their Clan.

In a War, there is no such thing as an old warrior, for if you lasted several battles the next one could kill you, if you were a skilled soldier you might last several years but the odds are defiantly against you. In the last part of the War of the Clans the Magic users deviled in all kinds of sick experiments using very dark magic. They did not know that they fell right into a Dark Lords plans to destroy all that did not worship the Dark Arts. At the time the Magic Users thought they had so powerful magic not knowing where it truly came from.

The reason that Daphne was not at the area of the camp was that she went in search for food, she saw several bushes that had berries close to their hide out and went to pick some. When she got to the point where the berries are, she started to pick when she saw this bright light. The next thing she saw was so huge and majestic figure there was no mistaking the features of the Forest God who stood before her. Daphne went straight into a prone position to show proper respect to the Forest God before her, until she shone the proper amount of reverence to her God. Daphne humbly asked the very large figure before her as to what she may do to serve thee my lord. The Forest God waved his massive hand in a motion as to come with him, and then the next thing she knew they were transported to his volcano crater home. He spoke as to why he intervened on her behalf, for if she stayed by the bushes she would have been discovered by the soldiers and killed after they had their way with her. The Forest God said it in fact, to believe him for he knew what he was talking about. Daphne wanted to ask him as to how he knew of the soldiers being there but thought better of it. She could not help looking around at all the beautiful items that decorated the home of their God.

He spoke as to what he wanted her to do for him, after Daphne wanted to ask why me? But held her tongue for she was still in awe over the fact that she was in the same room with her God. He spoke in a way that sounded like music in the air; he said that normally he would not ask someone of her abilities, to help him. But her mother was busy, and besides, he vowed to keep her safe while her mother was away with her own problems. How may Help you my Lord? Daphne said with all the respect that she could muster all the while she was freaking out about being around a God. The Forest God Spoke in a tone that made you feel peaceful and safe in his crater home, he went on to tell her what he needed of her and how she was to achieve it.

He wanted her help on a couple of projects that he was working on, you do not have to worry I will not put you in jeopardy but you will be working with me for a while. Time moves differently in here you will only be gone for a couple of days, outside you are in your own time. He went on to speak, then as a second thought he said that he will tell her mother that she was safe and not to worry. I will need you to help me with a list of things that you are going to recover for me. You will be receiving special powers, some of which may last longer than others and some will be permanent all of which you will know how to use. He then had her close her eyes as he reached for something from a cabinet near his left side, now child you will feel powerful magic flowing from me into you. Do not worry for you have the powers inside of you I am just releasing them so you are able to perform the list of things you will be recovering for me. Nothing that I ask you to do will have anything to do with stealing the items. All the items that you are going to bring back to me are in places where time has forgotten about and no one will be able to see you. For you will be moving outside of time and will not be seen by anyone or thing. Here is a map with all the items locations pointed out and what they look like. You will be carrying objects of a magical nature and an invisible pouch that transports the items straight back here. Remember all the powers that you now have will be yours someday, but for now you are immensely powerful as far as your magic goes. All you must do is to think of someplace or someone and you will be there, be careful in the future and use wisdom to keep you from getting in trouble. Do not let anyone know of your new powers for they may cause you harm, for they will look at you as thou you are some sort of how do you say? It is called a freak. Now I will have to go, for your mother needs my help to get her out of the jam she got into. Many of my people will see their God today and change the way they believe by the time I am done.

Go to the first place on the map and start along your way to the end of the list of items on the map, on the back of the map is where they rest and how to retrieve them just as a reminder if you forget. Daphne was left standing there by herself with this incredibly old piece of paper with a map on it, I better get moving on my quest to recover the items for she did not know how long it would take. Now to try out her new powers, she looked at the map, and spoke that she needed to go to the first spot on the map, without any smoke or any fanfare she found herself on a small island. Wow! That was cool she could not believe that she would someday have so many new powers, her own Mother did not have this much power, was she more powerful than her mother? Who knows, now I better get back to my mission at hand, which looks like a golden apple? It is to be found on the island close to here on a golden tree, so I better get it and go on to the second item on the list of things from her map.

She remembered what the Forest God said that no one would be able to see her thankfully for if anyone moved into any of the areas on her map this mission could get hairy. She walked in the direction that the map said and after a short while she ran into a town with many people and at the heart was a great Golden Apple tree. What are all these people doing here? For the Forest God said that the items where were people had long forgot? Well it is a good thing that no one can see me, for if they could she was going to be in big trouble if she picked the Golden Apple right in front of all these people. She decided to wait until there was not so many people around just in case something went wrong, after all no one was supposed to be here. That map was old looking, and if this was going to be so easy why did she need all her powers to achieve them? Well I better get this Golden Apple off the tree before she loses her nerve and must explain to a God why she had failed. The Forest God said that no one would be able to see me, and I hope he is correct for I would have a tough time explaining this if she got caught.

Even thou she was in another time that kept her safe from being seen she could not help but sneak around as thou she was stealing something and did not want to get caught. For this was the case and lord help if this plan goes wrong and she is stuck on this land in the middle of nowhere. Well here goes nothing she walked up to the tree, looked around to see if anyone saw her, then took a Golden Apple from the tree to put it in the bag. As she put the apple in the bag, she felt something grab her arm, as she turned to see what had snagged her, she saw the tree had grabbed her. What is this now she is caught by a tree that will not let her go, she pulled and pulled with no avail. If she did not get out of the grip of this trap someone was going to catch her just by seeing that the tree had caught something and was not letting, go. She decided to try to talk to the tree and see if it was just a built-in trap or was this tree able to capture people and stopping them from taking its apples. She decided that it was too big of a chance to talk aloud to her captor, so she tried a Mind Bump to see if it indeed was alive as we were alive that is. She concentrated on the tree and searched for its mind to speak to it as thou it was indeed something more than a plant. What came back to her in her mind was a combination of words and pictures, it was screaming at her to give it back the Apple that she took. She explained that she did not know that it was alive in the sense that we were for the trees from where she came from where just trees. She explained to the tree that she did not mean any harm to it in anyway and that she was sorry, but she needed her "Apple." To help save her world for an unbelievably bad God of evil and wanted to destroy their world and that her God sent her on a mission to bring back a list of items that he needed. The tree said that if she just asked her for an apple that she would have let her have an apple. But now it was going to cost her something that she needed before she could go with the apple, the tree had always longed to see the sea and for a punishment Daphne had to grant this wish. How was she going to get out of this?

She could just use magic on the tree to let her go, but that would not be along the Sage way of doing things and if her mother found out she would receive much more of a punishment then what the tree wants. She decided that her god must have known of this tree and was using it to test her in some way to see if she would do the right thing. Daphne must be going thru a test by her God to see if she would do the right thing or use magic against a harmless tree to steal its apple to get it and destroying a beautiful Tree with Magical Golden fruit. She decided to do the right thing and do as the tree wished and take her punishment for not finding a better way to achieve her goal. She asked for forgiveness for not thinking and stealing its Golden Apples, after that she explained what she was going to do to get her down to the beach to see the ocean. The Forest God told her if she wanted to use her magic all she needed to do was think of what she wanted, and it would happen. Well here goes nothing, she thought of the Tree with the Golden Apples growing feet of bark and pulling them out of the ground. She waited for something to happen to the tree in front of her hoping that she said the magic correctly. Then she heard a rustling, looked at the tree with the apples, and noticed the dirt moving, "please God let this work." With a glow that must have lit up the sky if it was night, the tree moved for the first time in its life it pulled out limbs fashioned into feet. The tree pulled hard and with a quake it moved one leg and then the other. The tree started to twist about with the happiness that it felt to be free of the spot that held it prisoner for so long. People were in the square when they heard the ground shake and the great tree that sat in one spot for so long moved of its own accord. The tree was so thankful that it bowed toward Daphne and then headed toward the sea to see the ocean that it wanted to see so much.

At this point Daphne thought it would be a good place to make her exit, but she could not help thinking about the tree. Will it be ok on its own or will the towns people hunt it down and kill it for thinking it be possessed, or will it return to the same spot to live out its days. Either way she hoped that all would turn out ok, but she had to get these items before it is too late, and the Dark Lord takes over everything. So on to the next place on the map and hoping that she was doing good and not messing things up to badly.

CHAPTER VIII

Back at the Forest Linda the Night Sage and her friends were fighting for their lives for if they could not get things cleared up with the council. She and Tree Mender and Gretta were all in trouble for trying to rescue a friend and a Spotted Horned Netter from the Dark Hoard. It all started when Linda the Night Sage went to the Forest God to see if there was a way, he could help rescue her daughters mind from the Dark Lord. And Tree Mender who came with as her bodyguard was forced to work for the mercenary Army that was marching by so as not to get captured and killed. Simple right? That is what I thought and never expected to in the Council Chamber a prisoner fighting for her freedom and her rank in the Sage as well. When Linda got to the point that she took an oath as a Sage not to lie to any of the people under her control. The Forest God decided to make an exceedingly rare personal appearance in front of the Council members and all to see him in his glory. With the appearance of the Forest God in the council chambers of course everyone stopped what they were doing and bowed down to show their humbleness before there

God. It is good that they still worship me after all these years said the Forest God, after a short amount of time the Forest God asked that they rise. The head of the Council was usually Gretta the High Sage and the forest god motioned for her to take her normal place at the head of the Council.

After that he requested silence from all the Council and all the people that poured in at the hearing that the Forest God in the Council Chamber. I have come here today to talk to my people and to clear up a matter that a friend of mine is in. At this there was all kinds of noise at the Forest God came to help a friend, he did not mean Linda, did he? Was heard and some disbelief over the forest God coming to talk to them in person, with all that is going on and he can find the time to talk to his People.

The Forest God raised his hand for there to be silence and the room became instantly quiet, now for the reason that I came here it is twofold for I came here to encourage my people to pray more than ever for there are going to be many hard times ahead, but if we stick together we can defeat any evil. Do not let others influence you and get you to turn your back against me for we will have to do many hard things in the future, and we need our people to stay unified. Upon hearing these words everyone in the room let out a big roar of commitment to their God and they all prayed together and after he listened to his people's fears and worries for the future. The forest God spread out his massive arms out and a piece came over his people and they knew from that point on, they could do anything that he asked, and everything would be ok. Then he addressed the Council directly about what they were trying to do to Linda the Sage and her friends. And how things happened, and that they were all under his protection and that there was no wrongdoing done in this rescue of a friend and the help by someone that was just trying to help a friend. He himself had given her the very item that she used to free her friends. So, with all that said he recommended that the Council adjourn and be done with this mess. With no one in trouble, and the fact that the Forest God himself came to defend Gretta and her friends, there was apologies said and they were free to go about their business. The

Forest God left in a puff of smoke and went back to the project that he was working on, the fixing of the locks of the Dark Ones prison. He needed the items that Daphne went to get as soon as possible and so he checked to see if she delivered any of the items on her list. He was happy to see the first item had made it to him with out to much trouble he hoped that map was quite old.

I hope things did not change too much. Daphne was reading the map and how to get the second item on the list, while planning for any problems in advance. She was not going to make the same mistake twice, and with that she thought about where she wanted to be and with a little magic off, she went.

Linda the Night Sage and her friends were all off the hook with the Council, but they may have some new enemies the way they got a God to defend them, there had to be some animosity. Not everyone there would be happy about being put in their place even if it were by a God. Good thing she was good friends with the head of the council, the High Sage Gretta and her being the next in command does not hurt either.

They all laughed at her joke and understood the underlining meaning behind it. All most forgetting, about someone left waiting Linda used the Mind Bump to tell Flaawna that everything was ok and to meet us at the front gate. And off they all went to meet Flaawna at the gate. So, no one would get the wrong idea or wonder why a rather large cat just walking thru the gate on its own. Linda could just see it in her mind, a giant cat walking thru the gates and someone sounding the alarm thinking she was hunting them or something. Flaawna may just get a kick out of it and scare everyone to the point they called the guards. Tree Mender was glad that no one was going to executed for treason or some other trumped up charge, he would have never thought that the Forest God himself would come to their aid. Gretta cleared her throat to get their attention. Now that everything is over there is a matter or some certain items that needed to be returned to the vault including the Time Devise as well for safe keeping. I expect that the items in question from the vault get returned after you ketch up with Flaawna then back they go Are we clear on this?

I do not want to explain to the council that the items were not returned properly. It was such a good feeling when friends get together for the greater good and are rescued for any wrongdoing by their God. What a day we all had! I am glad myself to have all this mess behind us and to know that everything will be ok. By the way. The Forest God and I talked via the Mind Bump and he said that he rescued Daphne and that she is safe and will rejoin them soon after she completes a task, I asked of her.

Daphne landed in the spot that the map pointed out, as she looked around for the next item, she spotted incredibly old ruins and walked in the direction of ruins. When she was close enough, she saw that there was a long passage that was pitch black, she thought to herself that this place is booby traps and that she better be careful. She decided that it would be a good idea to use some of her newfound magic to light the way. She could just use her magic to teleport herself to the item but that could be more dangerous for she might run into a wall or a trap or something. The item that she needed to bring back was a Chrystal statue of some type of long-lost bird. So, after gathering up her strength to go into the very dark and scary place she thought of a lit torch and one appeared in her hand. So no better a time then the present she said and walked into the cave thinking of a spell to ward off traps just in case of any trouble.

After what was hours and a hundred different turns, she was very lost, and was afraid that she may never get out of this place. When around the next bend she saw something very shiny lighting up the whole room that had to be the item that she was looking for. It was sitting on a pedestal in the middle of the room, someone must have thought very highly of this statue to make a shrine to a bird that no longer exists.

She thought to herself that she needed to check for any traps. Then a bright light came out of her fingers as thou they wanted to look around, so she did just that. No bells or whistles went off, so she figured that everything was ok, so she went ahead forward and before she grabbed the Chrystal Bird. She checked for a threatening message warning not to touch it. Not seeing any words or any message not to do what she was about to do, she reached over to grab the Chrystal Bird and it is eyes opened and tried to bite her. No way! This blooming bird is alive, that was defiantly going to make things a lot harder.

Daphne found out why there are no traps for the bird was a trap and she would have to talk it into going with her, she decided to take the easy way out and asked the Bird its name. My Name! What Are You Doing in My House? It yelled. She decided that the effortless way was not going to work so on to plan two. She spoke in very soothing words that her name was Daphne and that she meant it no harm, had you been asleep all this time. The Bird Yelled Back at Her "Of course not I only took a nap." I think you must have been put under a spell, for this place is in ruins and it looks like no one has been here for an exceptionally long time.

That cannot be true for I am worshiped by my people and they would not leave me here for all that time. The bird words drifted off at the end as though it was saddened by the thought of it being alone. How could this be I remember just yesterday this place was alive with people and the whole city was thriving? By the looks of it around here it does not look like they abandoned you, I think they all died off and you are the last of your kind. With a tear in its eye the Chrystal Bird flew off its perch and flew off to see for itself, after a brief time it returned saddened by the loss of its people. You were telling the truth for I flew all around the city and there was no life anywhere. How could this be?

What could have happened that they all are gone? By the signs of things, I was asleep for a long time as you said. Daphne approached slowly so as not to make a situation worse, she said that she was sorry for the Bird and that she did not know what had happened. The bird just stared at her for a long time, and then said its name is Christolarious and I was worshiped by my people for my magical songs. That healed as you listened to the beautiful tones that I sang to ease their pain and slowly made their pain go away. That is why their worshiped me for my beautiful healing tones, he said as he faded back to a better time when he first arrived at this place. When I first came to this place it was thriving with people as far as you could see, now they are all gone she repeated.

I did not mean to be in this place, but I was injured and one of the villagers took me in until I recovered. To pay him back for his generosity I offered to cure his wife who was dying and only had a short time left with us. I sang the most beautiful song that I ever sang, and the elders of the village came over to see what was happening, for they heard my song and was overwhelmed by my singing. After a while, the whole village came to hear my song and noticed that they felt better the longer they listened. Everyone rejoiced for their aliments were gone and they song out praises toward me for I had healed the whole village, which was much smaller at the time. The villager that took me in was shocked by the effect that my singing had on everyone. He was even more amazed by the touch of his wife's hand on his shoulder and turned around to see her fully cured of her illness. That man was my friend for the rest of his life, and I truly enjoyed his company for he was the kindest person that she had ever met. With nowhere for it to go, and the fact that her God asked her to bring the bird to him, she decided to ask nicely if the bird if it would like to go with her. The Chrystal Bird named Christolarious began to cry again at the realization that everyone that she knew was gone, they worshiped me.

Now this girl wants to take me home like I was her pet! To Christolarious amazement Daphne seemed to read her mind, "I don't want to take you home or anything." I thought with no one left to worship you, you could come with me not as a pet, but as my friend. You said that you had a villager as a friend many years ago, so why not try it if you do not want to stay with me that is fine. You are free and the last thing I want is to imprison you or hold you against your will, or in a cage. There are many people in my village that would love to hear you sing, I bet you miss singing before a crowd of people that appreciated your gift to heal. For we are about to enter a war and there will be many sick and dying people in need of your gift to heal.

There is an unbelievably bad Fallen God called the Dark One, that wants to take over everyone and everything nothing will be safe if something is not done to stop him. He has an Army of Mercenaries that grows each day with evil men that want to destroy anything that is good and destroy the world that we all live on. I do not mean to bring you into a war that you may want nothing to do with, but we all need to rise and take back what is ours. He will not stop until everything is gone and destroyed, no one will be safe from The War of the Gods. With that said Daphne went to leave for she wasted enough time and needed to return to the items on her list. She did not want to remove this beautiful creature by force or against its will, so if it did not wish to come with her on its own then so be it. She turned back towards the Chrystal Bird that touched her heart and said if you do not want to come with me that is fine. But could you escort me thru this maze of corridors to where I came in Please, I do not think I could navigate it alone. They looked at each other and could not help but laugh of course I will escort you out; this place is no longer my home and if just reminds me of what I lost. So, if the offer is still open, I would like to take you up on your offer, besides, it sounds like you may need my skills. I could use a friend, and do you had anything to eat I am famished I cannot remember the last time I ate a delicious meal. Daphne was hungry too, they had some food and spend the night here and then leave in the morning. Christolarious came out of the ruins and spread out her transparent wings and flapped so hard

Daphne thought she might break, uh I mean that she will get hurt, God I hope she did not hear that. Her Chrystal friend was having fun swooping and diving all over the sky, it felt so good to get out and just fly, she thought to herself. And then her hunting mode kicked in for she saw what a good dinner and the fight could be was on. She may not have flown in many a cycle or two but boy she could fly Daphne thought, she is so beautiful you can almost forget she is a real bird, not any old bird for she is defiantly a bird of prey.

With one final swoop she would either have dinner or she missed, and it was still a good hunt, she could always get more, one last fast pasted dive and it will be mine yes, I got it. Man, this is the best dinner I had in a long time; my mother and I were living on berries for the last couple of solar days. Boy do I miss my mother and my friends, man, I am so glad you decided to come with me, for I would be lonelier without any one to talk to. Daphne slept well that night for she knew no one would get past Christolarious, for nothing ever gets past her for her eyes are always searching for danger. They both slept soundly, for they thought there was no one else around, and had not been for over a hundred cycles or more. But they were not alone, for they were being watched by someone that would love to have such a prize as a talking Chrystal Bird. Lord knows what else it could do, he said as it looked, I will have to wait just a little longer to get my prize. Daphne woke in the middle of the night for she thought she heard something, or someone nearby, she decided to stay up for a while to see what was out there. She was stoking the fire when she heard a blood curling scream that only one Bird could make. Daphne ran over to the last place she saw Christolarious, only to find a glass bird that was by the look somehow under a spell, for she was as dead as the glass she was made from. Daphne had no idea what had just happened to her new friend but from that point she stayed awake, so no one had a chance to finish off her friend or her. Daphne had very little sleep since the attack on her friend.

Christolarious in the early part of the morning but she had to get the next item on the list, she put her in her food satchel that she brought with her everywhere she went. Daphne pulled out the map to see what her next item was and where to find it, she was getting more use to her powers and with a flash she was off.

Daphne had no idea where she was but according to her map, she was close to the next item, so she had better get on with it. The item was a cat and by the way her luck was going this cat was going to be trouble, well maybe she could prepare for any problems that she might run across like, lighting a torch for it would probably be very dark in the cave. She went to the cave and looked around for any signs of trouble that may cause her any issues like bones or fur like something would be living in the cave. With nothing interesting at the mouth of the cave she walked into the cave with no idea what was ahead of her for even with her torch she could hardly see her hand in front of her face. The cave took several turns and twists and she was getting lost, and a little scared. Suddenly there was a rustling in her bag God help me it something crawled into my bag, she was very scared now, she opened her satchel and saw her friend awake and herself again. Owe me! What happened to you Christolarious are you ok? She was acting as thou she had wakened from a bad dream; she said that she had no idea as to what she was talking about. And why was she stuffed into her bag, like dirty laundry? I thought you were under a spell or something, for the other night you cried out and then you were on the ground not moving as thou you were dead. I had no idea what to do? But I did not wish to leave you there where someone could make off with you, I was so scared that someone had cast a spell on you and I did not want to be the next victim. Well I do not have any idea what happened but why are we in a dark cave? I am looking for a cat that is on my list of items to bring back for him to use in aiding him to stop the Dark Lord that I told you about.

What you are collecting items for your god? Was I to be one of those items that you shipped off to your God with no care to ask me how I felt about it? I should of bite you while I had the chance. Well yes but I had no idea that you would be alive at the time, besides when I found out you were in fact alive, I knew it would be wrong to throw you into a sack.

You bet your life you were not putting me in any bleeping sack, even if it were to save the world. I am sorry that I did not tell you all the details why I was here, but it is very important that I get the other items on my list. I do not know ahead of time if any of the items on my list are alive or not when I set out to recover the items on my list, but I am learning as I go one at a time. All the items on the list are unusual and very old and that is why they are so important. Well we had better get on this you next item before anything else happens, my eyes are far better than yours if you lower your light I will guide us to your next item, let's just hope it does not protest to being put into a bag. You are never going to let me live that down, are you? Someday but not any time soon, you need to be reminded that no matter what kind of creature you find it has feelings and you should not forget it. Back to the job at hand, there seems to be several doors ahead I hope your map gives you the answer to as witch door and if it is locked or if there is a trap to look out for. I looked at the map earlier and it said nothing about a group of doors, yet alone witch one, I can use magic on the locks to see if there are any traps. I guess we can start with the first door and work our way down the line, you magic had better by good for I do not need a forty-foot cat thinking I am lunch said Christolarious. Keep up the wise cracks and you will find yourself in a bag, bird Daphne said with a smile, you would not dare came the reply from the bird. Well we have better pick the right door or we could wind up in some one's bag for their supper or stew. With that Daphne started to find out if the doors had any traps and how to decide the right door so they do not get into a fine mess. Daphne decided that it may be best to use a spell on the lock, so they could be out of the way if something went wrong. They would be far enough out of the way, and hopeful not hurt in the process.

Daphne wanted to try a spell to also view into the rooms one at a time to see if it was the right room, but she had never done so and had to think of the best way to do so. With the help of Christolarious they produced a way to see inside the rooms without setting off any traps and how to find the right room so they can find the cat that she was looking for. The map did not say anything about the size of the cat or if it was alive, so they needed to be extra careful when looking around for they may overlook it. They decided that they did not have that much time and so they went one at a time until they were to the last door. Her idea was working good so far, for they had opened two doors and looked all over with no sign of a cat, they were running out of doors so they decided not to worry about looking for traps and to just open the doors and look around. It was the last door that they found a closet door that led down a group of winding stairs. To be safe Daphne used a protection spell so they would be ok if something happened, also Daphne lit a torch, so they had lighter and down the stairs they went. The bottom of the stairs there was another door, so they cautiously went thru it and to their amazement there it was. This statue of a cat that was made of stone sitting on a pedestal, as they got closer, they noticed there was a sign on the statue.

They could not read it for it was in a long-lost language they did not know they both looked at each other wondering what to do about the sign. Try some magic on it and see if you can change the writing into our language of something. Something spokes to her and told her to read the words and they will appear in the language of her people, so Daphne went up to the sign and the word changed instantly into her language.

The words said: This Cat is the sacred vessel of its people and upon reading these words she will come alive in the form of the Stone Cat. I do not know how you did that thing about reading the word on the statue, but don't you dare say those words, we have no idea what could happen if you do?

Daphne got out her bag of teleportation and went to put the stone cat in the bag, but upon trying to pick it up she found out that it was too heavy for her to lift. They would have better luck with putting the bag of teleportation on its head and pull down the bag until it is all the way in the bag Christolarious said. So, with no better idea of her own she decided to try it, it may just work, Daphne went to put the bag over the head of the Stone Cat when someone entered the room. I would not do that if I were you! You may not enjoy the outcome from doing if you do so. What? Where did you come from? We are not here to cause any trouble; my name is Daphne and the bird's name is Christolarious we did not know anyone was here. The man said that his name Valorous and I am the keeper of the Cat which is sacred to my people, and you are trespassing on our property. Daphne knew that it was not going to be that easy as just sticking a bag over its head; we mean no harm to your people or the Stone Cat. We are on a mission from my God, The God of the Forest to bring back several items that he needs to stop The Dark One from breaking out of his prison. The Dark Lord has been trying to break out for some time now, and if we do not get these items that he needs the Dark Lord will take over our planet. Breath child for you were talking so fast I had a tough time keeping up with you. You said something about a bad guy was trying to break out of a prison? Yes, that is about right I guess, but he is not a "bad guy" he is the Dark Lord, he was a God himself. My God is trying to fix the locks on the prison that he built to hold the Dark Lord over a thousand cycles ago. Over a thousand cycles the Dark One built up his powers and broke one lock at a time until he could influence people outside of his prison to do his bidding. If he gets out, he vowed to destroy all the people that put him in the prison and then take control of everything with his Dark Horde. So as you see we need your help in this matter and you can see we need your Stone Cat, if you wish you can join as in our mission and bring the Stone Cat with you.

Valorous said he would need some time to think about what she had told him but did understand their need to gather up the items on her list. Just as we were about to leave, I received a message in my mind, at first, I did not know who it was from and then she introduced herself and spoke clearly that her handler was just being overprotective. She would love to help our cause against the Dark Lord, but she had to have her handler come with for her protection, and to care for her needs. She went on to say that if she would show her where the Forest God was living, she and her handler would be on their way. I went over the way to the Forest God's creator and said thank you, I said that I did not even know her name. She responded by showing me a random number of pictures and said that she over the years has been called various names, but she could call her Cloriese. One day they would be able to talk more but for now they had to get going I what she had said is true there was no time to waist. Her handler picked her up off the podium with truly little effort which was amazing for she could not even lift Cloriese she must be very heavy but not to him. Off they went and I had another item checked off my list. Man, o man she thought that she had struck out and that she was going to fail in her task, but everything worked out just the way it was meant to. On the way-out Daphne looked to see if Christolarious was with her so she could tell her about the next item, which is when she realized that she was not with her. Daphne went back into the last room to see Christolarious was talking with the stone cat and she wondered what was going on. When she entered the room, she heard them talking and Christolarious asked if she could travel with them to the Forest Gods creator. I was shocked by what I heard and wondered why she no longer wanted to travel with me? Had I done something wrong? Christolarious saw her look on her face and flew over to her shoulder and spoke in her ear, you have done nothing wrong and I hold no grudge against you.

You did such a decent job at selling the need of the Forest God and your people that I realized that I need to go with them to help your God and your people if I can. When you put it that way it makes sense for you to go, if was just a shock to find out you wanted to leave is all. Daphne will miss her Chrystal friend and she said her goodbyes with a tear in her eye. Linda the Night Sage was back in her rightful position as well as her co worth's, she is working to keep the Dark hoard from breaking down their gates. The High Sage Gretta was working on ways that they could evacuate the forest members, and how to get them there. Tree Mender was working with the Forest Guards is help reinforce the gates and preparing weapons for the Forest Guard to use. For they were mostly for show of force since they were used in the Thousand Cycle War. Or as it is better known by the Clan Wars, yes it has been that long since they were needed, they needed to be trained and fight if it came to that. The younger Sage in training had their classes cancelled for the duration of the war and were helping by making arrows that would hurt someone but not kill. The toughest part was trying to keep the town's people from getting into a panic over every little thing, so the Council were put in charge of handling the complaints since they needed something to stay busy. The War was coming to their front gates and by the God's they would be ready, Linda the night Sage was so busy with her daily work.

That she forgot about the God from one of the clans coming to visit with her and ask her about the plan to bring the Gods together. She prayed that the Gods of the Clans could put aside their petty differences and work together to defeat the Dark Lord. Daphne was helping the Forest God search for items that he needed to repair the locks, and she knew Daphne was safe, but she missed her daughter.

She hoped that Daphne and all her friends would not see the things that a War brings, the stuff that can harden them. I had the worst dreams for many a cycle from what I saw and heard was enough for anyone, she would hate for her daughter to go thru what she did. From what the scouts come back with the Dark hoard was getting bigger every day; witch meant that the Dark Lord saw still influencing people and that the locks are not yet fixed to hold him in for the rest of infinitely. Linda was not looking forward to the task that only Gretta the High Sage could approve, they needed to get into the vault to see what could help them in the upcoming War of the Gods. Only Gretta and the Council had the authority for someone to enter the vault, and she was not going to ask the Council after the last time, while it was still fresh in their minds. She could not hold off any longer, she had to set up an appointment with Gretta, one of which she nor Gretta were going to like one bit. At that moment she heard the unmistaken able voice of her friend Gretta in her head. Gretta was quite fond of Daphne's Mind Bump; you were looking for me? I heard that you wanted to talk to me, you know you do not have to set up an appointment to see me. You can always reach me in my mind, or did you forget about what your precious daughter gave as a gift to the sage. No, I did not forget what Daphne did to save her mind and in turn created New Powers for all the Sage to use freely. She is going to have many more Powers that she will bless everyone with for she is not one to hoard her Powers if she could share her powers with as many Sage that could learn. Linda spoke to Gretta in her mind and she let her know what she had in mind and what her role would be. Gretta was surprised that she would even try to get into the vault again so shortly after her last infraction, but she was right. She agreed that they must have excess to the vault and that they had to go thru the proper channels this time, hopefully the Council would see it the way they did.

They had an army coming right at them and being a peaceful Clan, they only had a small amount of solders called the Forest Guard. The Forest Guard was first formed in the Clan Wars that lasted over a thousand cycles, but after all these cycles with piece they are now just a small group of one hundred men. Tree Mender has taken it upon himself to gather more men and to train them properly. The younger Sage in training were making arrows and doing all the odd jobs that are not getting done by its normal Sage for they were pulled for other duties. Linda the Night Sage did not have any more visits from any of the Gods of the different Clans, and to be truthful she was worried that they may not overcome their petty differences. The Sage are all busy with all the preparations that were needed to get ready to defend their Forest from the Dark Hoard. And the Dark Lord himself, there was no way she could leave for any amount of time at all to see what is going on outside of the Forest. Linda was starting to worry about her daughter Daphne for she was helping the Forest God gathering items to fix the prison and the locks that hold the Dark One at bay. Gretta had told her that she would contact the Council and get an emergency meeting; they had so much to do until the Council could be gathered for session how could they get it all done? To find out exactly what is going on at the Hoard encampment they needed a volunteer to go over to where the Dark Hoard is and spy on them. There is only one person that she could trust with such a mission, but he was needed here to train the Forest Guard that has been idle for way too long. With so many cycles of piece no one bothered to make sure that the men were being trained properly, and so they had not trained since the last War. She would have to trust Tree Mender to pick the right person for the job; she prayed to her God that he would be able to find the right person in time.

The General of the Dark Hoard was furious over the loss of his prized stead, the cook that was helping by washing dishes. What was his name? Ah yes that is it Jonny Long Sword, he will have to be killed for being a spy for one of the Clans, he was so pissed about how easy it had been to infuriate has Army. The worst part he had to find another stead for the upcoming battles he was a General for God's sake. He joined his Army at the spot that he had told them to wait and had a very loud talk with his Captions about spies. And how they better get their acts together if they wished to stay living and holding on to their rank, each person joining would have to show their credentials, or they would be killed on the spot. He wanted to find out what progress they had made since they were camped at their location? Then how they needed to beef up security around the camp, for if they could not keep out spies how in the Dark Lord's name where they going to win against the remaining Clans? Part of the Dark Lords plans were to keep the Clans separate so he could kill each one of them, one at a time, for they were weaker that way. The Dark One was getting increasingly closer to breaking out for good, for he was not going back in that prison if he could help it. He had just a couple of locks to go and then he would be free to destroy anyone or thing that got in his way. He could feel the Forest Gods efforts to keep him in his cell, and he could also feel he desperation, his feeling for those Forest people were going to be his downfall. With the Dark Lords power growing more powerful each day the Forest God was working around the clock; he was outside of time in his crater home. This helped him for he could work much faster outside of time; he was in a time bubble where time did not change, but one solar cycle per one hundred solar cycles outside of his time bubble.

He was working so hard and so fast that he did not hear three guests asking for admission into his normality quiet crater home. When he investigated his viewing glass that he used so as no one could enter without hid knowing about it, he saw a Stone Cat his handler and a Chrystal Bird. We request entrance for we were sent by your messenger Daphne she said that you needed us to help overcome the Dark Lord and his Dark Hoard Army. We came from far off and we would like you to let us in and give us what we need to recover from the rough trip. The Forest God was pleased that Daphne had come threw but why had she not used the portal that I gave her? The Forest God found out very quickly why she had not used the portal for the items that he had on his list were not alive the last time he needed to find them. They were "magical" items that must have evolved into what was before him now; the Bird is very talkative and has strong ideas for a crystalline creature. He was not expecting this when he sent Daphne on her quest; I hope that she is not having any problems collecting the other items. Just then the bird introduced itself as Christolarious. And then she did not know anything of her past up to the time Daphne tried to grab her and stuff her into a bag. She was very shocked to find that all her people were long gone and there was no one left of the great city that once worshiped her. Christolarious was so devastated by this news that she had to see for herself if her people were all dead as Daphne said they were. Her temple is ruins, and everything was long ago lost to some catastrophe that she was somehow saved from. That is where the handler for the Stone Cat said his name was valorous and his companion was Cloriese and that they both were at his will and will help in any way possible. Great the Forest God exclaimed we have no time to lose so we had better get to work. You each have specific skills that you own, and I am going to have to push those skills to the limit, but not to worry I will not cause you any harm. So, without any more delays they got down to work on the problem at hand, now all I need is for Daphne to keep up the excellent work.

Daphne needed to speed up things on her end because the Forest God needed every item on the list as soon as possible. He sent her a mental message: for her to keep up the clever work, but they were running out of time, so please work with all diligence. She will receive it in no time at all for he did not use her Mind Bump but an unusual way to communicate all together. Some day he would teach it to her mother so if she needed to find him for any reason she could do so right away. He needed the other God's to come together and combine their powers soon for it will at some point be for not if the Dark Lord gets his way. I got the perfect idea to address his need for the help of the Gods and he had just the right messenger Christolarious. He would have to send his message to the other Gods and while he did that, he could get her to stop talking so much. My Chrystal friend I need you to send a message to the other Gods and you must send them my message of need to come together so we can defeat the Dark Lord for the last time. I will attach my official seal upon each letter to the Gods, so they know that you are my official messenger. They will be extremely hard to convince for there is bad blood between them as well as jealousy over who was the strongest and who should be number one. With that information in hand Christolarious flew the direction for the first God on his list. The God of the Sea and water had a name, but she did not know if she should call him by his name or not? His name is Orcefious and is not known to be very friendly you could call him more of a loner if you can call a God that? She decided to wait and see how things went, as to what to call him for now. But she had to think of a clever way to get this God to realize far more at jeopardy then he thinks and that every man and God are needed. To gather to defeat the Dark Hoard and its leader the Dark Lord, the sooner they can get things ironed out the faster than can concentrate on the bigger problem at hand.

CHAPTER IX

Before she left the Crater, he did a Mind Link with her and gave her all the information that she would need to bring around the other Gods. Thanks to the Link she now knew everything about all the Gods and the history between them, and where to find them in their fortifications were, they lived out their daily lives. She was properly prospered for the task at hand and she had the mouth to get it done, even if she had to play dirty, and bring up something, or someone they wished to forget. Gods were known to go around dressed up as a Wardarian and find someone that they could, we will let us just say have a night on the town. The Demi-Gods were even where known to have children with the servants that worshiped them. These children are known as Demi-Gods for they have the attributes of both their parents, but they were not pure Gods.

She had no wish to upset a God to the point where she will become a pile of Chrystal pieces on the ground. So, she planned on just using what she would need to get them to help, she may be loud, but she is not stupid, a whole city worshiped her at one point in her life. Boy how things have changed from the years of being on top, then the next moment you are a delivery boy to the God's. It is not so bad when you put it that way "delivery boy to the God's" sort of sounds good that way but she would like it more as "delivery bird." So, with her mood changed a little she went on flying to her first delivery point of Orcefious the God of the Water Clan.

He is not the worst of the God's, but he does like his peace and quiet and does not like to by disturbed, he does the calling not the other way around. Well I hope that first he is in, and second that he is in a good mood because weather he likes it or not, I will be there soon.

Christarious liked flying at one time before she was turned into a Chrystal bird with powers of healing.

She was just like all the other birds, but her Mistress wanted something different as her pet, and by magic I was reborn into what you see today. Life has been good, not to complain, after her mistress died of old age no one knew what to do with me. So, before the getting was bad, I flew out the window of her room and flew with my crystal wings for the first time. I flew and flew until a spotted an island with people on it and flew on down to a well in the center of the courtyard tired and very hungry.

Yes, I still ate from time to time, but mostly after consuming many long days without either one or the other, the rest you know. Thanks to the Mind Link I had the right information as to what part of his complex to approach so that I drew as little attention as possible. I did not want anyone stopping me from seeing the Water God; the only problem is my terrible memory which may be a problem down the line. Well I guess that I will address that when or if it becomes an issue, now I must find an open window to fly into, so I do not need to use the front door. For a God this may not seem over the top but to a mere bird this place is majestic, all the gold alone was a sight to see. Then you have all the jewels that are so shiny that you could get blinded on a sunny day, do not even get me started on the rest of the grounds. Back to the problem at hand, finding an open window to fly threw that will get me to the heart of his home for lack of better words. At last she spotted a window that was open a little bit but too small, but she had to try, or it could be hours looking for another window that was open all the way. She had to make a try of it and hope she did not get stuck, or worse caught and put in a cage. For a God that did not like visitors, he sure had enough a lot of staff to take care of his, well every whim which was going to get me caught for sure.

Now if I could just remember the way to his inner chambers, where he should have been at this time of day, sitting there receiving his lunch, not too much pressure. I had no idea that it was so hard to be received by a God in his home if I had I would have asked for back up. She should wait until after lunch so as not to disturb his lunch with a problem that he just had to help, and it was up to her to talk him into it. Hell, he will be mad by my disrupting him in his solitude anyway, so I need to get on with it. After all the fate of our World depended on this plan working out so he will have to just get over it. Just as luck would have it, she remembered that there was a back way into his chambers that would be for the staff. For them to come and go, so they were not going in and out the front doors of his chambers for staff could not be seen popping their heads in and out, for it would be considered poor educate. She just had to time things right so that she could get into the back stairway and back out without getting caught. She still had not worked out what she was going to say to him so that he agrees to help them, and she could get to the other names on her list. She was having great luck as far as to getting thru the back stairs without getting caught, right up to the point where she came around a corner and ran smack into no other then Orcefious himself. She did not know who was more shocked herself or the God that she smacked into, but he was not going to let anyone know it. Good thing that she was being so sneaky, or she may have made a bigger mess, not. With a look of shock on by face after nearly knocking him over he must have seen something in my wide eyes for he told everyone to leave the room and that they were not to be disturbed. I apologized to him for running him down like that, but she was afraid that you would not see me if I came thru the normal channels. My name is Christolarious and I come with a plea from the Forest God asking that all the Gods put aside their differences. And unite to make a difference in how this "War of the Gods" was going to play out.

The Forest God apologies for not being here himself but he was busy trying to hold together the locks which keep the Dark One in his sell. He is working at a rate only a God could work at to construct new locks that would be able to hold him back at least another thousand cycles. The forests God commissioned me to preside and to ask if you could look the other direction when it comes to any grievances you may have against him. For the good of the whole so that the Dark Lord can be dealt with and put in his place for an eternity. You are the first of the God's that he approached with his plea on behalf of all involved for you are pivotal to our plan and with all your help we can pull this off. As you are aware the Dark One has grown to the point that if we do not strike first there may not be another chance. With you on board with his offer of piece and the coming together of all the God's there will be a greater chance to defeat the Dark Lord. Before you give me your decision, please think of the

greater good and of your people for after he has defeated the Forest God he will be going of the rest of the Gods. We all know that he will never stop at the defeat of one God for he wants to take over all that we hold dear and destroy the planet while doing it. The Forest God implores you to except his offer of piece among the Gods to defeat an enemy that endangers every one of us. We have no time to wait for the sooner we act, the better chance we stand at defeating him and his Dark Hoard. Just remember that once the Dark Lord is free from his prison, we will not be strong enough apart to put him back in there possibly more dead than alive. I cannot leave here until you give me your answer for without you the other Gods may not join our little war party. The faster we move on the Darkness that is trying to take over everything that we hold dear the better the outcome will be. So, can we count on you to save our world and its entire people?

After the War, if you want to go back to your old ways of solitude than that is not a problem for that is your right. Things at the Forest compound were about as bad as things could get, now the Dark Hoard is camped just outside of artillery range and we have guards standing watch twenty fours cycles a day. Tree Mender is doing his best at whipping a bunch of old tired solders into crack fighting warriors, if they only had more time, but the gates could be stormed at any time. We do not know what they are up to and all our spies wind up dead in front of the gates not but a couple of hours past suns down. Communication had been cut off due to the blockade that is stopping all travelers from reaching the Forest compound things have to get better soon. When did our beautiful Forest become a compound anyway? That just does not sound right no matter how many times I hear it. I miss my daughter and pray for her save return, I pray each day that she is safe and success in the work that she is doing to help save our way of life. Things just do not seem right without her bright shiny face and her way of getting in trouble about each moon rising and I would hear it from one of the councils that she was up to her old tricks. I am writing this journal to keep a record of the daily events, so someone can know what happened to our once beautiful World. I pray that we win in this War of the God's but right now it does not look particularly good for any of us. This is Linda the Night Sage and my hope is that any future races that visit whatever is left of our world. Would have an exact picture of what a majestic world this was before a lust for power pulled it apart. Excuse me, sorry to interrupt you while you are busy, but we need you in the Council chambers there has been some news that affects us all. Well I guess I will have to see what has happened; I pray that it is good news for we all could use it about now. Do not worry I will write every detail in my journal for you to read about it, well I must go.

When Linda walked into the Council Chambers everyone was standing up from their seats and shouting at each, Linda could not stand the noise of all the council members shouting all back and forth at each other. So, she put a stop to it and with one loud whistle she got everyone's attention, what is going on here? How dare you act in this manner? We are Sage, we are better than these are we not? Everyone sits down and let us talk out our problems like the way you Sage do when in the

Council Chambers. Now where is Gretta and why is she not here as head of the Council? Will a Sage in training please see what is holding up Gretta, with her absence I am in charge and now let us go as Council should and one problem at a time please. Now what is first item before us today, "man this is going to be one hell of a day Linda thought to herself?" That is when the Sage in training came over with a concerned look on her face, "I went to look for the High Sage like you asked, but she was not in her rooms and no one has seen her since yesterday"

What? Where could she have walked off to? She did not have time to search for her right now she had the council's problems to deal with. Tell no one that she is gone just yet, she may turn up after a while, that will be all for now, thank you. Just what she needed was another Sage gone when she could use the help, she will use a Mind Bump to find her later, and she hoped nothing has happened to her. The council was in a panic about the blockade and how we planned to take care of it, so the traders can get their pelts for their traps, and then there was one thing after another that needed to be fixed right away. The blockade was the biggest problem and not for the pelts but for everything they needed. All Their crops, trade replacement, solders, and many other things that are too many to count on one hand. The blockade was a very real problem that needed to be fixed sooner than later if they we are going to stand a chance in this war.

But how are they going to achieve that with an army camped out at their door. She just hoped that The High Sage Gretta was safe and unharmed, for she had been trying to reach her for hours now. Linda had even used the Mind Bump it was flawless unless that said person is too far away, then its abilities are far less than perfect. With everything that is going on here with the blockade at the large army just out of our gates she just wished that she let me in on her plan so I would not worry.

Linda was putting all her efforts into finding a way around the blockade that she was startled out of her thoughts by a very loud boom. Linda ran to see what was going on outside of her window and saw the darnest thing, she ran outside to see Gretta with this large devise that was belching out fire. Gretta informed me that what she had in her hand was called "Dragon's fire" and that was why she disappeared without a word. She not only got past the blockade, but she was able to bring in a weapon that the answer to their prayers. Gretta informed me that the Dragon's Fire was able to affect a large area with a flame that gets hotter and hotter, until it engulfs everything in its path. That is all great but how do you put it out, if we spill it while trying to attack the blockade and burn down our Forest in the act? Yes, it is dangerous; to handle but if we launch it into that blockade nothing will be able to put out the fire until it devours everything in its path. One do not have much of its components that make the actual "fire" part and the ingredients are exceedingly rare. With the right timing at night may just blow open a big enough hole in their forces we can get all the men and supplies and men we need? This may only work on them once for if we try it more than once, it may backfire on us and work in their favor with just a little work on their part. Let us pray that this works in our favor and buy us the time that he needs for the Forest God to fix the locks on the Dark Lords prison. Hopefully, this will be the last time that he is able to weaken the locks and tries to escape, just maybe this will be the last time we have to deal with him and his followers.

Daphne only had a couple more items to go on her list of things that the Forest God needed, I problem that she had was the list kept growing.

She would think that she got the last item and there would three more new ones on the list. The Forest God told her that she was outside of time and so the time it took her to get the items was far less than the time everywhere else. Most of the items that he needed were not willing to go into the bag that she has that transported them straight to the Forest God's Crater. Some were troublemakers and had to do things in a different manner then she would have liked. One of the items that he wanted went down on an early sea vessel and I had to hold my breath the first couple of times that I had tried to retrieve it. And then I would remember that I had all kinds of powers that would make the job a whole lot easier. The one thing that would have to be changed next time, if there was ever a need again that is, would have to be the way to transport the items back to the Crater. If I knew more about my magical powers, I could just transport them there myself, but I was not brave enough to try it. The kind of trouble that I could get in if I transported something and it did not arrive at the right place. I could not live with myself if I did the magic wrong and something terrible happened like the time where I cause my choirs backfire on me producing a "bat bear" or something like that. No one was around to bail me out of it like when that happened, and boy did I learn my lesson with that mess. Well back to the task at hand what is the next item on my list and where will I have to go to get it, I think I have been to every out of the way place left on Wardaratia. Great it looks like I stuck my foot in my mouth of this next one, for it looks as thou I am going to have to travel outside of our realm for the next item. Well it is a good thing my map explains how to get there and where the object is, by the look the size of this thing it is going to be the hardest one of all.

Yes, even harder than when I had to remove a tree in front of a whole town without causing a riot, because it had Golden Apples on it making it well loved. I need to stop stalling and get the next item on the list, boy do I wish I had someone to talk to, I never thought that I would miss Christolarious. I have a feeling that this one is going to be one of the

hardest one out of all of them, for according to the description this thing is huge. Better get on with it, good thing that I have powers for I may need all of them on this one. Well not all but going to take a while to figure this one out as how I am able to get it in the bag. I hope nothing goes wrong on this trip, but if it is anything like the others it is going to interesting, that I know for sure. She focused on what she wanted, and she was instantly taken to the exact spot on the map, well it looks quite so far, hope it stays that way. Is this the right spot for there does not seem to be anything around? She double checked her map and that was when she saw some incredibly old script on the back, she could not make it out, so she decided to try magic. That was the biggest mistake she could have done, for it now read "do not tamper with" do not use any method other than asking the map to translate. About then she noticed that it was a protection spell to protect the map from getting used by anyone that was not given permission to have the map by its owner.

The map started to glow and then she was in a small dark room in chains attached to her wrists and secured to a very solid wall. Boy I really am in a jam this time, how in the name of the Forest God am I going to get out of this one? How are you going to get out of this mess Daphne? That is when someone walked into the room threw a door, she swore was not there a minute ago. Walking toward her she reached out for the map that she still grasps in her left hand forcefully and demanded how she got it and who was she working for. I am sorry I did not mean any harm.

I am looking for an artifact on the map that can help save my planet from a Darkness that is trying to take over all that is pure and just.

Silence Girl! I will let you know when to talk and do not try anything tricky, for those chains you are in will repel magic of any kind. I am the protector of this "artifact" as you called it, and no one is going to pop in and remove it while I am around to stop them. My people have protected the statue of our greatest wizard, for just before he passed on, he imbued this statue with all his powers. He vowed to return from the grave and lead our people into a whole new generation of power and wealth, with peace throughout the lands. I am the last of my kind and I will protect his statue until his return or my death. It is written that in a time of great need he will return to reset the hands of time forcing out anyone that is unclean and evil at heart. That is what you tried to remove from this spot and for that breaking you will hang here until to end of time, or the statue comes to life freeing my Master. My name is not important, but you should know my master's name since you admitted to practically stealing his vessel to use for whatever it was that you came here. His name is written in every book that my people ever wrote for he not only created us he also brought us here to live our lives in safety, to prosper as we meant to from our birth. You look like you are not from around here so you may not know his name but from this day forth you will never forget it. He is called by many names threw out time and space, but my people knew him as the "Creator" or Magus the Powerful to his people. A prophecy from long ago, when my people were still plentiful, speaks "of a time when he will return in the event of great need to overcome any who threaten his people." I am the last but when he comes back, he will restore his chosen people, to greatness, to live out time as he sees fit. In part of a prophecy called "The Traveler" speaks of an outsider coming with a worthy cause that will mark the return of "the Creator," but that surely cannot be you for you are but a child?

I can be called a traveler for I have been given a job by my God, to find things threw out time and space to help build new locks.

To hold back the Dark Lord from escaping from the prison he has been in for over ten thousand cycles. How could this be? I will have to check the Great book of Prophecies to make sure you are the one spoken of by our prophets. And if you are not you have a lot of time to hang around regretting your poor decision to come here and steal our Master from his chosen resting place. This prophecy is my only hope to get out of this by the Forest God please let her believe in her own prophet's words. Since she did not know how long her captor was going to be gone, she decided to make the best of her time. She looked around the room for the map, to see if it could have any other words of wisdom that she may have overlooked in her haste. There it is on that table in the far corner of the room, great it may as well be on the other side of the planet. She could use her magic to bring the map to her, what did she say about the chains? "That if I tried to use any magic against the locks that they will repel magic of any kind." Yes, that is it, but she never said anything about using Magic on anything else. I can stand a fair chance of getting out of here in one piece with a little luck and a lot of magic. It was about then that the statue of the Creator started to make this very loud noise that could be called a signal to prepare his people for his return. And bring them running towards the sound to see what it was. They all knew of the prophecy of his return and glorified in the coming of their Creator. It worked for the person that described herself as the last of their kind run into the room wondering what I did. I did nothing it just started on its own, your Master is about to make his appearance, or the statue have some alarm attached to it to stop people from taking it. You were right the first point, my Master is coming home to make his people great again, and plentiful for I cannot continue going on as the last. His plans for his people will renew our once great people back to its former glory, his name will be known threw out every land.

As Daphne saw it, she this could go particularly well, and the Master will help their cause or get very mad that she would not ever get down from this wall. Either way she had to do something to improve her odds and now was as good a time as any, she had decided that she needed to wait for the Master to appear and take her chances with him. She was the one that the prophecy spoke of that would bring the "coming of the Creator" was she not, things looked she just fulfilled the prophecy of his coming. Now the ball was in her court as to speak for she had her adversary at a disadvantage for how you can argue with long dead prophets. It looks as thou you should cut me down before your Master sees that you have the one that brought him back to you is in chains. I know I would not want to be the one to piss him off in the first minute he is back. Get Me Down Now! Before I have you flogged for your disobedience all signs show you who I am or wait and see what happens to you if you do not. Your choice, but by the sound from the statue tells me that he will be here soon ether you could look great in front of the Master or be on his bad side. Yes, you are right about cutting you down, I still do not know if you are the one that the prophets spoke of but that can be decided later. But do not try any wrong moves or you will pay with your life, I must prepare for his coming. Leaving was the first thing that popped into her head, and then she remembered that she was sent here for a reason and she was determined to see it through. So, she waited for the Master to appear, at least she was down from that wall, so I guess it could be worse. After a while she started to wonder how long it would be until the Master would be making his entrance? All kinds of things ran through her head, like how it was possible for a long dead Wizard was able to come back from the dead? What caused the all- powerful Wizard to die in the first place? If he was capable of so many things why die and kill off all your creations in the process? What just to prove you could do it?

Being young she found it hard to focus on one thing for long, most of the time she was kept busy, so it did not matter as much. Wait a minute she was on to something? No way had this guy had all the power that he was claimed to have, or he would still be here. He had to leave for other reasons then that were written down in the history books. One question answered he was lying about at least one thing; I wonder what else was "fudged" about their Master? Just as she decided to put the problem to rest to speak, in walked the last of a long-known member of long dead race. She was dressed differently than the way she was just a little while ago, this must be the way the Master liked to see his followers. She was now dressed in what you would expect a high-ranking member of a temple priestess with the white flowing gown and all the jewels. If she ever got the chance, she had a growing list of things she did not understand, but for now she was content with watching what was about to take place. She spoke in a language long lost to this world, up to this point that is she did not understand the words but saw the effect it was having on the statue. First there was insignificant effect to her chanting but after a while you could see that the statue starts to shake and sway, the more she chanted the more it shook. As she looked around the area of the statue, she could see things start to fade or dissolve the air around it. Wait something was happening to the statue right before her eyes!

What is that?

The next thing Daphne knew was she back in the Crater home of her God of the Forest unharmed. Sorry to pull you out of their when I did it was about to get very unsafe for you and anyone around. Let us just say what was coming threw was not the Creator, but a very evil form of him that was left behind. What his magic protected him from, the Creator is long gone. If you had stayed one second longer it would have a link to this world where it could destroy another planet like it did that one.

We have enough evil in this world as it is, we could not handle any more, then what we are fighting now. Thank you for bringing me back when you did, or things would have ended very badly if I stayed one ounce longer. In the end you can never run from who you are, even if you do not like some part of it, you are who you are.

If you try to remove a part of yourself that you think is holding you back, in the end it will always be there waiting to come out. That young one is what killed the Wizard, he could not change who he was without continence's. I was hoping to stop the events that happened before more evil was released. But as I said you cannot change certain things, not even me as a God could stop Evil from happening, it is part of all of us all we can do is hold it. How many items do you have on your list? If you have not finished it, I would suggest you get back out there so we stand a chance to contain our Evil here the Dark One.

Chapter X

Tree Mender was having one heck of a time trying to recruit solders to protect the Forest and its entire people with this blockade of the Dark Hoard's. With over a thousand hired goons sitting camped in front of the North entrance makes it hard for anything to get in or out. So, without enough qualified solders he was forced to train anyone willing to fight for their freedom, and to defend the Sage who is their direct link to their God. Defeating the Dark Hoard was not going to be won on the battlefield if we could stop the Dark One in his tracks. And keep him from breaking out of his prison the Hoard will crumble without their leader for he is the reason for their will to fight. With no reason to fight and no one to pay them they will just leave the battlefield under their own free will. But they must be able to hold off the Hoard until the Four Gods can defeat the Dark Lord and keep him imprisoned for the rest of his days. Thankfully, Tree Mender has some incredibly good leaders of the now defunct Forest Guards who are more than capable of leading the New Forest Defenders. The God's must be successful in defeating the

Dark One and stopping him from influencing any followers from his prison. If they could somehow form a Magical Dome to preventing him from contacting or influencing weak minded individuals willing to serve him. Many People that he can pervert into something less than what they were in their daily lives. Monsters that will kill anyone or anything, without thinking twice to please their Master the Dark Lord, they are just a shell of the person that they once were.

These are the makings of the Dark Hoard that sits just outside our Forest home. They are no longer human, for the atrocities that they have committed in the name of the Dark Lord makes them much less than human. They must be stopped at all cost; to release them on our world would bring the end to the way we live. First, they needed to remove the blockade from the North end of the forest so we can get men and supplies flowing again. If we fail in removing it, they will starve us out way before the Dark One breaks out of his prison. Tree Mender meets up with the different leaders of the Forest Defenders to find a way thru the blockade. Away that they could get items and people across the blockade, under or around it, did not matter which way they used if it worked. They were having a challenging time producing a solution to their problem, Wait! Tree Mender was part of the Dark Hoard for a while (undercover) as a cook, and had a challenging time trying to get out alive. But if they could infiltrate the hoard Army, they might be able to sneak in some supplies and find out vital information about their next move. If they could get someone on the inside the Intel alone would be worth it, if they could get more than one all the better. What? You cannot be serious about sending someone from the Forest Guard; they will be spotted right away. They are not ruthless enough to fit in with the Hoard and will be killed on the spot. There must be another way that does not require our men dying needlessly, Can the Sage with the help of the Council produce a magical solution to our problem? After all there is a lot of things of magic in the Sage Vault that they could use. I can ask them to set up a special meeting with the Sage and the rest of the

Council members and ask them to open the vault and see if there is anything from the Clan Wars. Do you have any other ideas? If not you all need to get back to the troops, and work on their skills as they do not die the moment that step out of the gate. This was going to be one of those days, for the suns are barely full in the Red Sky that he loved since a young child. Now everything was in the Sages hands now, may the Forest God lead them to the right answer to their dilemma.

Gretta was not to overly excited about the problem of the blockade being thrown in her lap to fix again, for she had to go in front of the council not too long ago to get permission to use the Dragon's Fire. And that did not go over well the Council was in an uproar over it for the better part of a cycle. As the head of the council she had the final say but if she wanted to keep her job on the Council she had to do what the Council suggested more or less for if she did not what was the point of having a Council? So, when Tree mender brought to the floor of the Council his idea, she was not shocked by their answer that they gave him. The question of using some items in the fault had been brought up before, but if the items in the vault were safe to use, they would not be in the vault. Linda the Night Sage had taken some items out of the vault not long ago, and many on the Council have not forgotten that infraction yet. She got off too lightly as far as several members were concerned, they may have punished her more, had they had the chance. Thankfully, The Forest God stepped in to get her out of that jam, but without Him telling The Council what he wished done for now the case was closed.

Sometimes "what the Council does not know about" can get things done that would never be approved. It could not hurt to test some of the items in the Vault to see if they were safe to use in case they needed to be used soon. But who could she trust not to tell the Council members what she and Tree Mender were up to? Linda was the first to pop into her head, but she did not want to get her in any more trouble, after the last incident was fresh in their minds. But who else could she trust that had no problem with bending some rules to get the job done? Tree Mender had gone with her in this mess, so he was defiantly going to help, and she has no choice but to ask Linda the Night Sage for her help as well. They needed to get access into the vault without being seen by the guard, and then remove choice pieces to test somehow without getting caught, no problem. Right?

Well without to such effort Linda and Tree Mender got in and out of the vault with a little helping hand from Gretta. Now they needed a safe place to test the items that they removed without destroying themselves or the forest around them in the process. If there was a place nearby that we could test stuff without being heard? We may have to work at night for if we started to duck our duties during the day, they would come looking for us to find out why we are not taking care of our jobs. So, it sounds like it is going to be a bunch of late nights for a while, so bring plenty of Choocka Beans to keep us from falling asleep. If this was going to work, we must find an item from the Clan Wars that will get us thru the blockade and safely get us back. Do this without being seen, or by doing enough damage to the front line of their forces to keep them busy for a while. We could dig a tunnel under the Hoard and dig under their feet far enough that we could do so without being seen. Why did you not produce that idea before now? We could use our Shifting powers to fly over them, we could shift into a small insect and we could go over them unseen. That just might work if we could Shift into a flying insect small enough to not be seen, how about a Dragon Flee we cannot get much smaller than that. Dragon Flees lives on the scales of Dragons sucking out their blood and using the Dragons for protection from predators. It is settled then we will Shift down to their size and fly right over their heads, high enough not to get swatted of course. Now all we need is a place that is in the middle of nowhere that we will not be seen or worse heard. What if we use the Battlefield of the last Clan Wars, no one goes out there anymore? It sounds a little morbid going out there to test items from the Clan Wars that were last used in the Thousand Year War. But you are right it will be perfect for what we need to do, that way if something goes wrong one else will get hurt. So, they had the items, the place, and the plan all they needed now was to wait until things slowed down enough that they could sneak out.

They decided that they would test the items, they figured that they would take only a couple at a time that way if things got out of hand, if items start going off uncontrollably, they could handle it better. Less items to go crazy means less damage, it least that is what they hoped would happen, sounds good in their heads anyway. "We will have to wait and see what happened, hope everything goes well they could use it" said the Four God's looking down on them, "I try not to mettle to much in their lives, but sometimes the situation calls for it." "yes, we all agree on that, until they force your hand" sometimes it takes a God to get things done. With that they wise crack they all laughed aloud, it felt good to be able to bring the fellow Gods together without jealousy, or any petty differences thought the forest God. Ok enough spying and more working we have a long way to go on these locks and all most no time to finish them. He was going to need to find a clever way to thank Christolarious for getting all Four Clan Gods here and with no strife, "I hope she did not promise them anything that I am going to regret later." "Well whatever it is it will be worth it after we deal with the Dark One." Now if Daphne brings the last couple of items, we might just be able to defeat that pain in the Ass and keep him locked up forever. Back down on Wardaratia Linda the Night Sage and Tree Mender were just winding up their last of the days duties and were on their way to meet. So, they could go test the handfuls of items that they removed from the Vault. It was more than a little freaky coming her after such a long time trying to forget what had happened here. Everything came back to her in a big rush not only was she reliving what happened here, but she could feel the magic that was still alive in this place. Forever haunting these grounds making this Battle grounds inhabitable for the rest of time.

What Linda felt was the Old Magic that was poured into this ground over the Thousand cycle "War of the Clans" she felt it, the Evil that drove men to be slaughtered. Both sides of the War were present still in the grounds and she felt all of it flood into her as she stepped on the Grounds after One Thousand Cycles. The feelings were there, but how could it be after all these cycles the feeling of immense power wash over her repeatedly. Picking at her mind and to draw her into her worse

Nightmare ever, it is in the middle of the War and Magic was flowing so fast. Too fast for her taste and she started to feel extremely ill, but not from the spinning and turning of her dream, but of what was in it. There was a darkness that flowed over everything back in the beginning of the War. We all thought it was the work of the Dark Lord, but now she knew that it was much eviler than the Dark One could ever be. This Creature of Darkness fed on the Evil of others and has been doing so, for well over a millennium of millenniums it is the darkness that all other Darkness in the Galaxies were formed. The Evil that went ahead to come forth built up so great, that the pull drew, it here to feed on the hate and desperation of the soldiers, and Magic users alike. The need to follow Evil from the vastness of space to its point was too much for it to pass up. For years, it fed on the Pure Evil that, we fought to destroy, but it was not from the Dark One for he was a puppet to ensure its meal of Evil would continue to make it fat. Yes, Fat on our destructive force, the Magic, the Blood Lust, all of it was like sweet candy to this Evil creature. But this was his home for over a Thousand Cycles, and it had not been fed lately and is very hungry. The creature fed on so much hatred, anger, greed, blood lust that it was stuck for it grow so large it could no longer move due to its own Lust to feed on pure Evil. It ate so much of the stuff that funneled down into the ground that it was about to its breaking point when the War ended.

Now it has lost a considerable amount of weight over a thousand cycles, and it was hungry once again.

Things all make sense! She could now feel the creature that was trapped under the Battle Grounds of the War of the Clans. Linda felt the large amount of Evil coming from "the creature," her stomach turned, and she knew she would be sick if she did not run far away right now. At first, she felt like the one she was running in sand and then she felt the creature become weaker, and that is when she made her move. Yelling back to Tree Mender "to drop everything and to run," then he decided what ever could make Linda run the way she was then he should listen to her. The Creature that feeds on Evil is the biggest threat they have ever had, The Dark Lord was nothing when it came down to it, they had a much greater problem. She needed to see the Forest God right away and to tell what she found and just how evil it is, it did not just feed on evil, it was evil. Tree Mender just caught up to Linda the Night Sage when he noticed her become sick all over a poor tree. What is wrong?

And why are you taking it out on that poor tree, the look on her face made him sick just from the look of fear in her eyes. Tree Mender had seen many different sided of Linda and he had never seen the look she now had on, and never wanted to again his whole life. This was a side he did not think Linda the Night Sage even had, let alone would let others see, pure fear is about the closest he could come if he had to describe it. What could make her that scared that she would run from it as fast as she could? For a woman that is over one thousand cycles old she could really run fast it took Tree Mender all a quarter mile at his fastest pace to catch up to her. When he did, she was sobbing so hard that you would think someone in her family died. I gave her a little distance so she could pull herself together; only after a long while I came up to her to ask what was wrong? Linda something must have affected you in a bad way, to make you lose control like the way you did. After a short while she said in a whisper "you would not grasp what I saw without a Mind link" for she did not want to recall what that creature was like.

Besides, you will see exactly what I saw and heard when we were on the battle grounds, I never want to go to that place ever again. Tree Mender agreed to her using the Mind Link but was nowhere ready for what he saw and heard in her recall of the creature of pure evil. He felt sick to his stomach and did lose his lunch for the Mind Link was so vivid, as thou you were there standing next to her. After he recovered enough to speak, he said "no wonder you ran" that would affect anyone that fights against Evil her whole life. What are we going to do about a creature that is made up of pure evil? That thing makes the Dark One look like a slight problem; he must be under its control, a pawn controlling his every move. We must tell the Gods about this new problem that wipe out our entire race, I must go to the Crater and speak to the Forest God. I need to tell him about this new evil that is on our planet waiting to use anyone to fatten its self-up on pure evil. Go back to the Forest and carefully sneak back in and get the council to listen to you any way you can. Have them comb thru the records of the Clan Wars to see if there is any reference to an Evil stronger then the Dark One. Whatever you do, do not let anyone go anywhere near that Battle Grounds, we may be able to beat this thing, but not before knowing more about it. She had thought ahead enough to bring the one item that would take her straight to the Crater home of the Forest God pulling out the magical devise that was given to her by the Forest God, and instantly standing in his work shop. What is its Daughter Sage after my own heart? It had better be good as to why you would call on me in this time of need. We have a new problem and it makes the Dark One look small and inconsiderably small in comparison to what I just found in the Battle Grounds of the Clan Wars. Continue Sage or do I have to remove it from your brain myself, she said that a Mind Link would be a better way to tell him of what she saw. With that said, he did just that. That explains a lot! Now our focus is going to shift from keeping the Dark One in, to helping him out of his prison. What? You want to help the Dark One out?

Quiet Sage! You are in the presence of your God! And if I said we need to help the Dark One out, then we will do just that. Linda knew that she was in trouble for questioning the Forest God and wished to tack back the words. Linda apologized for her outburst and for the first time looked around to see all the Gods were shocked by what she said. Was it the outburst? Or the part about needing to release the Dark One from his cell, I do not know. She felt ridiculously small right about now and decided to let someone else do the talking. Linda the Night Sage sat in a corner seat far from where the God's discussed the News that she experienced firsthand. Then as out of now where, Daphne her daughter was right in front of her, she been on assignments for the Forest God but was called back since things had changed. She could hardly hold back the tears for she absolutely loved her daughter, and this was a perfect timing for her so needed a diversion. Talking with Daphne would be the perfect way to stay out of trouble; they had to keep it down for they did not want to disturb the God's at work. How have you been doing child I missed you so much and with the way things are turning out we will not see each other for a while more.

I will let the Tree God tell you about what is going on since your absence, but you will be shocked by what he is going to tell you, for sure. Now do not keep your God waiting you need to check in so we can talk later maybe at dinner time, for I know you could appreciate a home cooked meal. Her mother was right, protocol dictates that he receives the first news so here goes everything, My Lord I came as quick as I dare, I hear things have changed, but I know not what? Or how? Thank you, child, now wait over there for a while until I finish with our plans to break out the Dark Lord. What? He wants to now break out the Dark One, all this time I was running all over the place to gather items to keep him from breaking out. What ever happened while she was gone must be quite different for them to break out an old foe, to do what stop a new one? No nothing from this plane is more powerful than the Dark one, beside the other Gods that is.

Things in the Forest have not gotten any better, they still had the Hoard outside their Front Gates, and then there was all the talk of a creature that is so much more powerful than the Dark Lord. Can things get any worse for our poor way of life, now there is talk about the God's producing a plan to break out the Dark One from his prison? What is that all about? Linda the Night Sage had been gone longer then he had expected and there are just too many questions that need answering. The Council is all over him daily; he is running out of excuses to tell the council and did not know enough to tell them more. Just as he was at his wits end, he felt the Mind Bump from Daphne that said she and her mother will be home soon. Tree Mender could not wait to see his friends and get some news at how things are going on the outside of the blockade. He knew how far Daphne was able to cast out her powers (at least he thought he did) so he waited for them to appear in the home of Linda the Night Sage. He fell asleep and was wakened by a loud noise that signified their coming home, he had fallen asleep for the first time in days. But how dare he not let them see him asleep in their house, for they will not let him live it down for a long time. He stood up as they were making their way to the outer chambers of Linda the Night Sage, and he was glad that he did. Linda was not in the mood for any lengthy welcome home from anyone but him. She was all business but under her rough exterior he could see she was glad to be home. After the congeal round of welcome home she got straight down to business, thank you so very much for waiting up for us she said in the most pleasant way. Now we have many things that need to be addressed right away, before anyone could get any sleep, Sweet daughter of mine what can you tell us of this present the Forest God gave you.

Daphne did not see it as a gift but more as a glimpse into what she was to become, she told her mother and Tree Mender of all the things she did on her adventure for her God. Do you know how much power that you own and how much of that is short term magic given to you as an awaking of your powers?

She told them as much as she could about her powers, but a lot of it she did not know of herself, it just comes out of her when she needs it. Some say that most magic comes from deep inside and when the time comes more is released as you grow into your powers. That may be true for most, but she is the only one to have powers of her kind since the Clan Wars, which makes her different in so many ways. Her powers come to her in greater waves, the more she uses them, and she has no way to determine the amount of her powers at this time. Linda thought that after all this mess is gone, she would run Daphne threw a bunch of tests to find out just how strong her powers were. They may have to put her powers to the test on the Hoard that is camped out on their front lawn.

Of course, as a Sage in training she cannot do anything that directly kills anything, or she will lose her powers before she has time to find out what they are. Linda knew if others are also gaining powers again, that the Dark Lord may be seeking them out for his evil means. If that happens, they are all doomed to repeat the past and by doing so making the same mistakes all the way back to the Clan Wars. Their only hope is to find a way to up route the evil that is living under the Battlefield and turning their biggest foe into their ally. But one or the other may be more then they will be able to pull off, unless all the cards fall right into their laps and at this time that seems far off. What we are going to need happen is that all the good forces and the Dark Lord and Hoard, to come together against a foe. A foe that could destroy them all and bring an end their world. Someone is going to have to be the mediator to bring both sides to the Piece Talks and lead the charge against the evil that wants control of their planet. The Gods of the Clans are working together for the first time in who knows how long, but what is to happen after this no one knows. The biggest thing is to get the Dark One out of his prison, and to realize that he was used, by "the Evil" from some world that came here to feed on our people.

Back at the crater home of the Forest God the plans are being made to free the Dark Lord from his captivity, and working out how to get him to work for them, in the up and coming conflict with the Evil beneath the old Battle Grounds. Working on the locks to try to keep the Dark Lord in was much harder than breaking him out, and so they were making particularly satisfactory progress. The four Gods agreed upon a plan to help their captive realize that he was used, and hopeful they will be able to bring him in on their plans to remove the Evil from their lands. They decided to set out to talk to the Dark Lord in his cell before they would let him loose if he cooperated and did not link up with his old partner. He was used but he thought that he could gain power over anyone that opposed him. The hardest part was going to be getting everyone working together without any animosity toward the others involved. And then after everything is said and done what was to become of the Dark One and all his followers. There had to be a way that they could all work things out for you cannot have good without evil, but everyone must come to some agreement after the War of Evil.

That is why the four Gods were setting up a ground of communication to keep this from destroying them all, that the plan of the Evil creature that invaded their planet. If that is his goal then he had done just that to many other planets, Lord knows how long it has gone from one planet to another destroying anything in its path. It must be stopped somehow and sent back to wherever it came from, never to bother us again, but how?

They must try to find its weakness, if it feeds on the Evil in all of us that is the way to stop him? Do not feed it or give it what it wants, if it is starving then maybe it will leave if it has nothing to feed on. The hard part is going to be how to starve it to the point it leaves or it is weakened to the point that we can imprison it; we do have one that we are not going to need soon. How hungry is it? How do we starve it without it taking another ten thousand cycles? These are the things that needed to be worked out before they can more on with any plan.

Somehow, we need to find out what the Evil creatures, weakness is and how we can exploit it to defeat it. The only way that I can think of would be to put it in a state of euphoria, or sleep so we can do a "Mind Link" on it and search thru its brain to find out more about it. All things no matter how Evil they are have some form of a brain to control its Heart, Lungs, or whatever else its body runs, so it does not need to stop whatever it is doing to manually control its body.

This creature said that it is pure Evil and that it was stuck under the Battlefield from feeding on our hatred during the Clan War and cannot get out. So if that is the case then it is not what it is said it was for it had a body and is wedged in a hole from eating too much of our Hate,

Rage, evil Magic, desperation, all compelling people to kill for way to long. It kept us at each other's throats to feed for a thousand cycles until it could not absorb any more. We need to act quickly while it is still in a weakened state and trapped by its own lust for Evil, and whatever negative feelings that brought it here from some far-off galaxy. Enough of this waiting for this or that we need to act while we have an advantage over it, now is the time to act and that is just what we will do.

Linda the Night Sage made a special session of the Sage Council for she planned to let them know about a plan she had and how she was going to attack the pure Evil creature. She had been doing some thinking and she had the start of a plan as to how to get rid on this thing for the last time.

Daphne was called away again, for the Forest God needed her and when a God says he needs you. You drop what you are doing and go to where he wishes you to be; thankfully, she was able to send her mother a message threw her Mind Bump.

She had an escort that had come a calling on her this time, an old friend Christolarious who was also doing work for the Gods. It is so nice to see you. How have you been? She also was glad to see her friend and let her know everything that she had been doing since they last met. She had been flying all over sending messages to this person, and that person, trying to get support for the up and coming fight with Evil.

A Creature that absorbs all the hatred, pain, malice, and every other Evil way, it uses all that junk to feed on. It came here to fatten up over Thousand Cycles ago and is now hungry again and is trying to pull our planet apart to get what it wants. We have no plans to let it do so now that we know what it is up to, we plan to fight it, but how we do not know yet? The Gods are working on it, but they need you to help with a very touchy subject, but I am not at liberty to say anymore he wants to ask you himself. We should be there soon and once we get there you have an audience with the Forest God, so if I do not see you again before you go, it was good to see you again.

Thank you, it has been nice to see you as well, she was going to thank the Forest God for sending her to be her escort. Daphne had an idea why the Forest God had called her back after such short notice, and it could only mean one thing. But she will wait for her God to fill in the details and what he wishes her to do, she just hoped that she could live up to what they needed from her. The Forest God called her into a small room in his Crater home and sat her down to ask her about the reason he brought her here.

He said that he had a plan to get rid of the Evil intruder that currently lives under the battlefield of the Clan Wars. Not only that but it claims to have feed on the hatred and all the raw emotion and influenced the length and how bloody it become just to make itself

What we want you to do is very dangerous but you can handle it, we want you to intervene and communicate with the Dark One and convince him to help us remove the Evil Creature, or trick him in doing it for us.

If he will not help us in this matter we are hoping that threw his greed he will help us without realizing it, we are hoping for the first part of the plan to work, and he helps of his free will. For his freedom will be granted if he can succeed in the task that we want his part of it, for let us be real about it we could achieve it a whole lot easier with his help.

Either way we plan on him being a major part of our plan, with his help or not, we will be counting on his greed to deliver the message we want him to tell the Evil Creature. I cannot tell you anymore at this time for we do not want to tip off either side about the full scope of our plans, if things go bad for you with the Dark One we do not want him to read you and find out all of our plans at once. So, will you do It? Talk to the Dark One and try to win him over to our side, at least we can try being honest first and hope it works. If you can get him to remove his Hoard from in front of the Forest Gates, your people would feel a whole lot better. But no pressure just be yourself and try not to let him be aware that you have any magic for he may not trust you after that. So, will you do it? Of course, I will, when do you want me to start?

Knowing what he is going to say was no magic for she knew he would say right away. So, when he did it was no shock to her system, but one thing she was worried about was being alone with him. At least at first until she could get a better read on him and weather, she would be safe, I have but one request that if something goes wrong could someone pull me out.

Of course, you will have a bodyguard if you think necessary, do not worry you will be the only one aware of his presence. The Dark One is no fool he will expect you to try some sort of way to protect yourself from a direct attack from him. We also have things set in place for you if you get leery just speak one word aloud and you will come straight back here.

The only question is whom you want me, as myself, or a strict, rigid negotiator that does not pull any punches, this is the way it is going to be sort. Well we do need this all to happen as fast as possible, but I do not see the Dark Lord going for the "this is the way it is going to be." Let us start out with your sweet side and if we must, we can try the other later, remember he is very smart so you will not be able to fool him completely. As far as the rest is up to you as how you handle, we the other God's and me will back you within reason, but you are in charge. Daphne wanted to laugh and crying at the same time, for no matter how this turned out someone was going to get hurt, she could see it coming. She was not looking forward to seeing her charge (The Dark One) for this was going to be one of the hardest things she will ever do. The way things were explained to her they were trying to deceive the Evil creature with the help of the Dark Lord being on their side. Or the Dark Lord going over to the other side and using him to trick the Evil creature while he is duped not knowing we would never trust him from the beginning. One way we get rid of the Evil creature that lives under our old battlefield and still have the Dark one to deal with. But if we pull it off the other way, he will hang himself and the Evil as well, getting rid of both. It was left up to her as to the outcome, but if you think about it, she has truly little control, and the Dark One has all the control he just needs to play out his role. We do not want to put you at more risk then you are ready for, so if you like you can talk to him from this side of the prison, until we know more how he will act. Always remember that he may just be biding his time to try to fool you into reveling what you know, so keep your walls up and do not let him trick you. And one last thing we talked to you about a safe word if things get to hairy, well it is "wonderfully" remembered you have to "say it" not think it.

There is saying "no better time than the present" so if you will arrange it, I would like to see him at your earliest convince. We all were hoping that would be your decision with time being so critical, but it will take a short while to set everything up. So as my guest please feel free to sit in my study or if you wish you can wait in the inner gardens. My personal favorite is the gardens and may soon be yours too, now I had to get things rolling as well as see to it you have some suitable accommodation. How about starting fresh in the morning and that will give us enough time to prepare for your mission. Also, that way you can produce a good plan as to how to approach your conversations with the

Dark One. So, you do not go in there and seem like you do not know what you are doing, you do not want to give him anything that he can use against you. Stick to the facts as to why you are there and you should be ok, remember he is not stupid so if he seems off in any way, he may be trying to trick you in some fashion. Now if you are hungry my cook can prepare you something to eat, or if you like, I can see you to your rooms so you can get a fresh start in the morning. Daphne ate a light dinner that was sent to her room and then, fell straight to sleep, not a fit sleep but more of a night mare, she was being tormented over and over by the Dark Lord that had her on a spit over a fire.

The more she fought the tighter the ropes got, after about the fourth time waking up in a sweat, she decided that she should cast a spell to protect her thoughts from anyone trying to intimidate her, in the subconscious part of mind while she slept. She had not prepared before she went to retire for the night, and the Dark Lord got into her mind. Or even if the Evil creature wanting to mess with her, knowing she would blame the Dark Lord either way she was going to shield her mind from now on.

Shielding her mind was defiantly was not their plan, but she was not about to make the same mistake twice for the next time it could cost her life. Her new motto was never getting caught with your pants down, she had to always be prepared for anything from now on.

After her restless night of fighting off bad dreams, she decided to get dressed and go into the main part of the crater home, she did not know if God's slept but she needed to talk to someone. She peaked around the corner to see if any lights were left on, hoping someone was still awake.

A lone figure could be made out in the chair by the fire, she approached carefully for he may be asleep, and she did not want to wake him if he was. Yes, young Sage could you not sleep or are you just up to relieve yourself? Come pull up a chair and join me by the fire you look cold, I can have something warm brought up for you if you like. Pulling up the chair closes to her she did as her God asked, besides that fire looked very warm for she had not realized how cold she was. So young one what is on your mind that you are up at this hour? Relieved that he brought it up first, she went on to tell him about her Nightmare and what she did to keep it from happening again. The Forest god just sat there staring at her with fondness in his eyes for he could see her growing in strength, which is good for she will need all of it before this is over.

Incredibly good you are learning faster than most your age, if you have any questions, I will try to answer them, when circumstances allow. For now, let us just sit by the fire and take in its warmth, for in but a few hours you will need all your wits about you dealing with the Dark One. Daphne was wakened by the house servant asking if she was ready for something to eat and a hot cup of tea. There is fruit on the main table until I bring your food miss, Daphne must have fallen asleep after talking to the Forest God, wow it was the best nights rest she ever had. After her breakfast she got dressed and prepared herself both mentally and physically for she as of now knew what preparation was very handy. She asked if all was for her to talk with the Dark Lord. Yes, was the replay, we are ready when you are, all safety measures have been put in order and are working fine. Well then let us get going for I wish to get this over with as soon as possible.

Daphne was escorted to a spot that from there they teleported directly to the front gate of the Dark Lord, traps and things were being put in place so she could safely converse with the Dark one. Daphne was also putting her own mental traps in place as well as blocking her mind to any unwanted probing to try to get into her mind to retrieve anything about her that she did not wish to share. Once to all clear sign was given, she was offered a chair to sit on so she could be comfortable, for there was no deadline to her first visit so she was going to make the best of it. She probed with her mind for the mind on the other side of the immense door that stood between them, she found a very powerful mind that tried to overcome her and send her out of there on a stretcher with her mind lost for all time. She was startled by the power that came at her that she fumbled for a minute and had to regain herself before any damage was done. Her walls of her mind were able to hold off the first assault but were shaken by the massive blow, she recovered quickly, for more faster than was expected and then they each knew the score. This one that they sent to talk to me mind is far more controlled them some that came before her, he was impressed by this one and he is never impressed by any mortal. Now that they tested the waters, and each knew a little more about the others powers it is time for the facts. He might as well find out more about why this mortal wishes an audience with the Dark One.

Daphne was not going to be bullied by anyone, but she knew how important these negations were, and they had to succeed to save the planet. She introduced herself as Daphne of the Forest people, for he would not be impressed by any titles that she had, so she chooses to keep things simple for now. But on the other hand, he was going to give her all his titles for he was proud of them and who knows he would impress her. After both sides introduced each other it was not time to start telling him why she was here and what she was willing to do for the good behavior.

The fact was that they needed each other so the quicker they can understand that the better, but Daphne was not that gullible to believe that would happen in one day. She did understand just how hard it, but she hoped that things would go well for the stake of them all. Each day was the same as the last getting nowhere and both parties were walking away more frustrated than before, until Daphne took control of the conversations and they finally started to get somewhere. The fact that he could not be trusted ever left the back of her mind, but she had to believe in the fate of their planet and that meant doing things the hard way. Until one day she just spit it out and laid down what was happening and what she was offering him. He thought it over for a minute and then asked, "do you have the authority to make that happen or are you just spinning my wheels." She was shocked by the openness of his question; she took a minute to think things thru and then replied, "of course I do or there would be no point being here." You do realize until you prove yourself one way or the other you will not be trusted fully, but we need each other, and a good start would be to call off the Hoard from attacking my people. Done! They will leave at once and fall back to await further orders, is that good enough for you? Yes, for now that will be fine thank you, hope to work with you soon on removing an Evil that will destroy even you. With that he threw back his head and laughed a very boisterous cry "we will see about that."

That was the being of us as a whole fighting for our planet, for whatever the reasons where we all were fighting for our freedom, and the way of our lives. The Days are all long and with bloodshed, but this is a War that we did not start but buy gosh we were going to finish it one way or the other. For that is one thing that we are is stubborn if we could live through a Thousand Cycle War then we can see this one to its end.

The days are all the same in a war you send out people to die and fix up the ones that are lucky enough to fight another day. The War that we are fighting did not go the way that we had hoped we were hoping to send all the Evil on our planet into a trap of our own doing. Yes, the Dark One did get out of his cage and prison, but he had other plans then being our "lackey" and went over to the side of Evil. So, we are fighting to rid ourselves of the Evil that is trying to control our world again, but at least the Dark One did one thing that surprised us all. He moved his hoard back and had never returned, so our Forest is free as we fight to free the rest of the planet.

The days all grow long with all the blood and loss we continue as thou we have for so many cycles. What was young is now old and nothing has turned out the way one might wish, Daphne did wind up marrying Tree Mender and they were happy until he was killed in the war. His son is just like his Father for he too wants to save the underdog, and yes, all the trees that he can. God I was hoping that my son Jerald of the forest would have a chance to grow up without having to go to the War that was destined to happen I see that now.

Time is short and I write these word with the hope that some will be left to read them, things are not going good with the War, we are all being enslaved by the Evil Forces that seems destined to tear it apart. The Dark Lord is now fighting the Evil for their Evil pact could not have lasted with so much to gain, we are slaves that feed and bath the Hoard. Our once great People are all gone as is the Gods, they have not answered any our prayers and they are no longer in the places they used to be. Some say they are dead, or captive by the Evil that is taking over our world, is there no one that will rise and lead our people back to our old ways.

This is the End of our way of life all is lost we as a people are gone nothing is left of our once brave people that lived in the Forest of our ancestors.

Now even that is gone, I am the last the Council is gone nothing stays but me, some days I do not remember my own name. This is the last time I will be able to write any more it is not safe with the Hoard rounding up anyone that is not enslaved already.

Wait where did that bright light come from? It cannot be. We may live yet, such a bright light it floods the sky and the darkness is going away. What could it be? Are we saved? And how, I am afraid to look but the Hoard is screaming in their death throws, what is happening must be an answer to some long-lost prayer. Could the War be ending, I do not know but I feel peace for the first time since the start of the War.

The End.